LOGAN

FEDERAL PROTECTION AGENCY

BOOK NINE

BY EVIE RILEY

Logan

Federal Protection Agency

Book Nine

LOGAN

A determined detective.

A young man's recovery.

**A break in a case that brings them both
one step closer to the truth.**

Detective Logan Hollingsworth moved to Baton Rouge as part of the Federal Protection Agency task force four years ago. Since then, he's been involved in taking down dozens of evil predators who commit crimes against children. When his most recent lead on a child trafficking ring coincides with an investigation of a boy who has been missing for almost a decade, Logan may just blow this case wide open.

Clay Dahler has spent the last four years living on the streets of San Francisco, doing whatever he could to survive. Kidnapped by a human trafficking ring when he was fourteen left him riddled with real-life nightmares. Clay has kept tabs on his older brother from afar but never contacted him. He feels too dirty and broken to go home. When a tenacious Detective crashes into his poor excuse for a life and convinces Clay his brother wants him back, can he muster the courage to take a chance?

Will the connection that blossoms between them survive as Clay's past continues to haunt him? Or will the link to Logan's investigation be the thing that finally tips the scales?

CHAPTER ONE

Logan

I SMASHED MY elbow against the doorframe as I dragged a struggling man across the room. He was shouting something, which I assumed was probably a lot of cursing, but the man was so drunk I couldn't make out a single syllable.

I let out a few curse words myself as pain shot up from my elbow and made my arm go numb. I'd been hunting this fucker down for days and I just wanted to get him behind bars and out of my life.

When the case came across my desk, I thought it would be simple. A man had broken into his neighbor's home and assaulted the woman and child living there. The neighbor had cameras and had reached out to the police immediately. There was no question about what had happened and who the perpetrator was.

Instead of the easy case I'd expected, however, I'd been given the runaround for days trying to find a damn abusive pedo who had seemingly disappeared off the face of the earth.

I'd eventually tracked him down to the basement of an illegal casino, which explained why he'd been so hard to find.

I none-too-gently shoved the man into the holding cell at the Federal Protection Agency's headquarters to wait for one of the locals to come collect him for processing. This was a part of my job I truly enjoyed, watching the assholes we caught shake and sit wide-eyed as they waited to find out what their fate would be after we tracked them down.

Don't get me wrong, as a detective I would never take it upon myself to dish out my own brand of justice and abuse the fuckers when we tossed them in cells, but I wouldn't treat them with kid gloves, either. That didn't mean I didn't *want* to beat the crap out of them, I just wouldn't. I prided myself on controlling my temper when faced with pedophiles and abusers. Some days it was beyond difficulty to resist, but I took my position at the FPA seriously and would never risk my job on the team just to get a few hits in.

I slammed the cell door behind him and shook out my arm to try and get some feeling back in the limb. The pins-and-needles feeling was just starting to leave my fingers when walked into the FPA offices. I plopped down at my desk and, with an audible sigh, pulled the top folder off the stack of waiting paperwork that never seemed to go down.

"Need some help there, old man," a nearby voice needled me.

Without needing to look away from my paperwork, I balled up a piece of scrap paper and tossed it at the man sitting next to me.

"Shut up, Roland. I'm only two years older than you."

"Yet it still took you three days to track down one fifty-year old pedo."

Looking away from the paperwork I'd barely started, I glared at my fellow detective. Roland slouched against in his chair, one elbow braced on the desk, and a shit-eating grin on his face.

Why was this asshole my best friend?

"Keep it up and I'm never inviting you over for another barbeque night."

"What? No, you can't do that." Roland leaned so far over his desk his arms extended onto mine, knocking my paperwork askew. "Tyler is on a new vegetarian kick. You're my only hope for getting any meat in my diet. You can't deny me. I'll die of iron deficiency, or something, and then you'll have to live with that on your conscience."

Rolling my eyes at my friend's antics, I returned to my work. Roland was a good detective, but I'd never seen him do any paperwork.

A miracle, and the luck of being the Boss's brother. I'd complain about the nepotism, if I wasn't personally aware of how hard Roland had worked for his position.

Plus, Roland's upbeat attitude was sorely needed in the FPA. Dealing every day with crimes against children could wear on a person's soul over time, and even the best agents and detectives were at risk of burn out. Having Roland around was like keeping a ball of sunshine in my pocket that could bring some cheer to even the darkest days.

I wasn't sure who he'd conned into doing his paperwork for him but my bet lay on the youngest member of our team, Drew.

Drew West, the son of Jonas West, a local detective with the Baton Rouge PD, and Cooper's new protégé. The kid was a wiz with computers, and after a bad start a few years ago when he'd gotten caught up in some black hat hacking, Coop had taken him under his wing and started teaching him the right way of hacking. Since Jonas and Coop had ended up falling in love while working on the case after Drew had been kidnapped and needed protection, the young man had plenty of time to spend with Coop.

In his new job of white hat hacking, Drew was working for the greater good, using computers and traversing the dark web to track down people like the asshole we'd just brought in. Criminals.

I was just considering throwing something heavier than a paper ball at Roland when my phone rang.

"Detective Hollingsworth speaking."

"Damn, Logan. You even answer your personal phone with that business voice? You really do need to get out more."

A wide smile spread across my face as I leaned back in my chair far enough to make the old wood groan in warning.

"Sebastian Roth. Holy hell, man. Where you been hiding? I haven't heard from you in forever."

An awkward silence echoed from the phone, and I could feel the weight of the other man's thoughts even from a distance.

"It's a long story. Did you hear about that pedophile ring that was brought down last month?"

"Yeah. It wasn't public news, but it was definitely the talk of the office for a while." I sat up so suddenly in my chair I thought the poor piece of furniture would collapse under me. "Oh, shit. Was that you?"

"Yep. Like I said, long story."

"I'll bet." The barely started paperwork glared up at me, waiting to be finished. I eagerly pushed it aside for the much more interesting conversation I'd found. "I'm guessing, since you're calling me and you brought up the topic, that you need my help with something concerning that case?"

"Sort of. It's..." Another heavy silence passed, this one even longer than the first. "...complicated. I'd rather not explain over the phone. Can you come by the office today?"

I didn't even need to check my calendar, even though I was fairly certain I didn't have anything scheduled this evening. Even if I had plans, Sebastian's serious tone would have convinced me to cancel them. "Yeah. I should be able to come over around six. I'll bring dinner. You still like that Thai place over by the park?"

"Yeah, sounds great." Sebastian's voice was fainter than it was before, as if he'd moved away from the phone or been distracted by something. "And Logan. Thanks."

"No problem. I'm always glad for an excuse to get takeout." I kept my tone as casual as possible, trying not to let myself get too worried before I even knew what was going on.

After Sebastian hung up, I sat staring at the dark screen of the phone for a few minutes, lost in thought.

The discovery of a major pedophile ring right in our own swampy backyard had been a shock, but I thought it was over. Baton Rouge's mayor had immediately set plans into motion to take care of the problem and make sure something like that never happened again.

So, what could still be worrying Sebastian so much?

"Hey," Roland tossed the same paper ball I'd thrown at him back at me, bouncing it off my head. "What's up? Problem?"

"I don't know." I shook my head. "I hope not, but... I really don't know."

CHAPTER TWO

Logan

ALIAS INVESTIGATIONS USED to be only a few minutes from the FPA offices where I worked. However, about a month ago Sebastian and Damien had moved to a different location. As I drove to the new location, I realized that the timing lined up with the pedophile ring they had brought down. The two incidents must be connected somehow, and I was already itching for answers.

I'd originally met the Roth brothers right after getting out of the Air Force. The young men were on the run from the Italian Mafia and in desperate need of some clandestine transportation. I owned a small personal plane, which I kept stored in a hangar just outside the city, and offered to fly them while keeping their names off the flight logs. Since then, they'd called on my services a few times, but this was the first time they needed my help as a detective rather than a pilot.

Alias Investigations' new address turned out to be on the other side of town, where property was much more expensive. It was an impressive building, but it only gave me more questions.

How had they afforded this, and why move in the first place?

All of those questions were immediately pushed aside when I stepped into the new office and was met with yet another surprise.

There were three desks. Sebastian sat behind one, and one must have been meant for Damien, but the third desk was occupied by a man I'd never seen before.

"Hi," I said as I sat the takeout food I'd brought on a nearby table. "I don't think we've met. I'm Logan Hollingsworth."

The unfamiliar man stared up at me with a stern expression, like he was a disapproving librarian, and I was an unruly kid that had dared make too much noise.

"Gabe Long."

I waited for further explanation, but none came. The man, Gabe, was completely stoic, as if his name alone should have been all the explanation I needed. I did vaguely recall hearing the name from Mason before in relation to some of the FPA's previous cases but couldn't place exactly which ones.

Sebastian stood from his desk and headed over to me, a tired smile on his face.

"Don't mind Gabe. He doesn't like to talk much, but he's been a big help recently."

Gabe's odd attitude was immediately forgotten the moment I saw Sebastian stand up.

"What the hell happened to you?"

Sebastian walked with a heavy limp, and with a cane clutched in one hand for balance.

"Oh, yeah..." Sebastian laughed as he tapped the tip of his cane against his foot, like he'd just remembered the state of his leg. "This is... part of the long story. Let's dish up that food you brought while its hot, and I'll tell you all about it."

A half an hour later, with the food mostly gone and the entire ordeal explained, I was left staring at Sebastian's injured leg with even more bafflement than before.

"A bomb? Really? They tried to blow you up? How did I not hear about this?"

"Bureau kept it quiet," Gabe said with a scowl that made his face seem even more intimidating. "Higher ups said a bomb scare would insight panic and told the news to report that it was a gas explosion."

After everything I'd learned today, being told that Gabe was an FBI agent who was "taking an extended leave of absence to consider his career" didn't even seem all that shocking. I'd also been forced to reevaluate my initial assessment of the man. Although he appeared intimidating and emotionless at first, he obviously cared about the victims of the pedophile ring they'd brought down.

Stacking the used plates and empty takeout containers aside, I braced my elbows on the table and gave Sebastian a serious look.

"This is a wild tale, but what do you

need from me. I doubt you called me here just to catch up."

Sebastian gave me a slow nod. "We've been busy tying up loose ends. All the kids we've rescued need to be placed in safe homes, and their families contacted, if possible, which is proving difficult when we can't even identify half of them. A lot of them were kidnapped as babies and don't even know their own names, let alone the names of their parents. It's slow work, but we're making progress. However, there's one loose end we haven't been able to solve."

From his pocket, Sebastian pulled out a picture and set it on the table for everyone to see. It showed a young boy with wavy blond hair and the biggest blue eyes I'd ever seen smiling up at the camera.

"This is Clay Dahler," Sebastian said as he tapped the photograph right above the boy's head. "He disappeared almost a decade ago when he was fourteen. His brother hired us to find him, but with everything that happened recently, our search had to be put on hold. We were hoping you could help us with this."

Lacing my fingers together, I regarded

Sebastian over the top of them.

"Why me? I'd love to help, but I work for the FPA. Finding missing or runaway kids isn't really our scope these days. Surely there are others more suited to this kind of case."

To my surprise, instead of Sebastian, it was Gabe who responded.

"Fourteen your old boy goes missing without warning, snatched with expert precision right out of his home, no note, and no ransom. There's only so many reasons for a kid to be taken like this."

"You think he was trafficked?"

Stringing multiple sentences together at the same time seemed to be Gabe's limit. He returned to his stoic silence, leaving Sebastian to pick up the explanation again.

"His brother, Jason Dahler, has been looking for him, and apparently tracked him here to Baton Rouge. For a while, we thought Clay might have been taken by the same pedophile ring we busted but... to be blunt, he was too old." Sebastian frowned.

"Too old?" I asked, though I had a sinking feeling I already knew what he meant.

"Out of all the kids we rescued from that facility in the swamp, the oldest of them was no more than ten. Clay was kidnapped when he was fourteen He would have been too old to be of any interest for this particular ring."

Sebastian slid the photo closer to me, so it sat only inches from my elbow. "You remember that case I helped you guys with two years ago?"

I instantly balled my hands into fists and ground my teeth together.

Two years ago, I'd been working a child trafficking case of my own. At first, I'd thought it was only a few people, but the more I investigated, the more I realized it was a much bigger operation than I first suspected. I'd been determined to bring them in, but they'd eluded me. I'd hoped that the ring Sebastian brought down was the same one, but he was right. His traffickers focused on a different age group.

If there was one thing I'd learned, it was that monsters like these were very particular in their taste and wouldn't suddenly change to a different age range of victims.

Forcing my teeth apart enough to talk,

I managed to spit out a few words. "That case is the bane of my career. Yeah, I remember it. Why?"

As an answer, Sebastian just tapped the picture on the table again.

When I looked back down, paying closer attention this time, I cursed.

The kid in the photo looked like a pre-teen boy, with blond hair, blue eyes, and face like a cherub that stepped right out of a Renaissance painting.

Clay Dahler perfectly matched the description of the other kids taken by the traffickers I'd failed to find. I should have realized it sooner, but I hadn't realized they'd been operating for so long.

Picking up the photograph, I ran a thumb over the boy's face, right along the seahorse shaped birthmark stamped on the side of his neck.

"You said his brother managed to track him here, right?"

Sebastian sighed.

"Sort of. The information is vague, so it's hard to say. This case is almost ten years old so any leads we could have followed on that angle are cold as ice now. Finding him might be impossible at this point."

"Give me whatever you got," I said, with a newfound conviction in my voice. "I promise you, no matter what, I'll find him. If I'd brought these monsters down two years ago, Clay Dahler might have been found sooner. I've already failed once. I'm not failing again."

CHAPTER THREE

Logan

A DISORIENTING ATMOSPHERE of loud music and flashing neon lights washed over me when I stepped into the club. Almost immediately, someone's hand slid across my chest and slipped inside the lapel of my jacket.

"Hey there," the flamboyantly dressed man said as they sidled up next to me. "Haven't seen you here before."

Their voice was hard to hear over the loud music, but they were slurring their words, giving the impression they were drunk, but their blown out pupils indicated they were probably on something harder.

Grasping the man's wrist and removing his hand from my chest, I pushed past him.

"Be glad that you've never seen me before, and I hope I have no need to see you in the future."

The words were a warning, considering the nature of my job, but I knew the guy would see it as a personal insult. As expected, he shoved me away, shouting "Asshole!" before storming back into the crowd.

I'd been to *Dinah's Place* before on several occasions, none of them for good reasons. On the outside it looked like a typical nightclub, but the backrooms were a different story. It was typical for clubs for dancers to take customers to the back for private shows, but this particular place used it as a cover for prostitution. As a rule, we usually turned a blind eye to it so long as everyone involved was consenting, and of age, but there had been a few instances recently where the "dancers" were of questionable age or were being pressured into something they didn't want to do.

I was barely there for more than a few

minutes before the owner of the club appeared in the crowd. Dressed in a short glittery gold dress, she looked more like a patron than the owner.

"What the hell are you doing here?" she said the moment she was within earshot, which in this establishment was only a foot away.

Dinah was a tough soul, older than she looked, and with plenty of experiences dealing with the law. Rumor was that she used to be a lawyer who got sick of playing by the rules. With how good she was at skirting the law, I was inclined to believe the rumors.

There was no bull-shitting her. The only way to deal with Dinah was to be as direct as possible.

"Do you really want to have this conversation here, out on the floor where anyone can overhear us?"

She glanced suspiciously at the dozens of people around us, who were all trying and failing to hide the fact they were eavesdropping.

"Fine. Come to the back office, but this better be worth my time or I'll have Jerome throw you out."

Jerome was the club's most fearsome

bouncer. At six foot five and two hundred and fifty pounds of pure muscle, he could easily pick me up and toss me out the door. It had happened before, and I swore I could still feel the bruises hiding under my skin.

As soon as the office door closed behind us, the noise of the club instantly fell silent. Dinah must have invested in some state-of-the-art soundproofing because I couldn't hear even a whisper of the chaos just on the other side of the door.

It also meant no one could hear anything that happened inside the office, but I tried not to think about that. I had a gun strapped to my hip, if necessary, but I hoped the situation wouldn't dissolve into violence.

Sitting in the chair behind her desk with the air of a queen, Dinah crossed one leg over the other, so the slit of her dress fell open up to the top of her thigh.

If I'd been into women, I might have been distracted, but I found myself only mildly amused by the attempt.

Frowning when she realized her distraction technique had failed, she tapped her nails on the arm of her chair.

"Right, you're one of *those*."

The smile on my face remained pleasant, though a little strained at the corners. "I hope you're referring to the fact that I'm a *detective*."

As she pulled a slim cigarette out of its box, she gave me a long, pointed stare. "Of course. What else would I be talking about?"

"Of course," I repeated. "What else."

Instead of smoking the cigarette directly like most people, Dinah first placed it into a long cigarette holder. She claimed it was to keep the smoke away from her face, but I suspected she just liked the aesthetic since she had at least a dozen different holders to match her favorite outfits.

She took several long drags, holding the smoke in her lungs for a moment, before breathing it out her nose.

"All right, Hollingsworth. What'd you want?"

Taking out the picture Sebastian had given me from my pocket, I slid it over to her. "His name is Clay Dahler. This is the last known picture of him, but he should be about twenty-three now. Rumor is that he may have been spotted at your club."

She didn't even bother looking at the picture, and I snatched it back before she could tap the ashes from her cigarette on it.

"I might recognize that name, but why should I tell you?"

Smoothing out the picture to make sure it wasn't damaged, I carefully stored it back in my pocket. "Because if you don't, I'll bring the DEA down on you. That patron out there who spoke to me was obviously tweaking, and they probably weren't the only one."

Her fist clenched hard around her cigarette holder, and she slammed the end of the long thin stick into the surface of her desk. It was made of metal, and actually managed to splinter the wood.

"I don't deal drugs in my club."

"No, you just deal other people's flesh. But you and I both know it doesn't matter whether you do something or not. The only thing that matters is if I can make a case that you do. If there's one person on drugs here, then there's probably more, and if there's enough, then I can probably make a case that you're dealing." I held up my phone so she could see it, with the correct number to my contact at the DEA already punched in and my finger hovering over the send button.

I waited, letting my silence communicate that my next move was her choice.

"Fine," she sighed as she pulled her cigarette holder out of the desk and brushed away the wood splinters left behind. "Someone named Clay Dahler did come to my club looking for work, but it was five years ago. I only remember him because he used his real name. Most people in this line of work go by an alias."

Five years ago, Clay would have been eighteen. Assuming the same pedophile ring I was hunting down took him, then the timing suggested he had grown too old for them and been kicked out.

But if that was the case, why didn't he go home?

Why was he still missing?

I almost slapped myself for asking that question, even if it was only in my head. The boy—a man now—had been held captive by traffickers for four years. There was no telling what state he was in, physically or mentally, and he probably wasn't thinking straight.

Plus, the traffickers had probably filled

his head with lies about his family, either claiming they had giving him up, or wouldn't want him back. I'd seen it before. It was a common tactic for keeping young victims under control.

I took a deep breath to get my emotions back under control, and nearly choked when I inhaled Dinah's secondhand smoke.

"All right. So, he was here. What happened?"

She shrugged, looking far too nonchalant for someone who had literally stabbed her cigarette holder through the table a moment ago. "Nothing happened. He wanted a job, but I turned him down. Eighteen isn't old enough to work here legally."

We both knew what she wasn't saying. Whether or not her workers were of legal age didn't matter to her. The real reason she'd turned him down was that he didn't look old enough to pass for twenty-one.

I was starting to piece a timeline together in my mind. He'd gotten away from his captors, either by escaping or being kicked out, and gone looking for work. Out on the street with no papers or official documents, getting a proper job would have been difficult, so he'd probably turned to the only work he knew.

"So, you turned him down. Then what?"

Tapping out the last ashes from her depleted cigarette, she stored the holder back in its drawer in her desk. "Look. The kid was scared. Obviously running from something, and from the way he was acting, it seemed like the people he was afraid of weren't far behind. I advised him to keep running and put some more distance between himself and whatever was haunting him. He used a computer here to book a bus ticket out of the state."

She paused, obviously enjoying my frustration and impatience.

"The ticket was booked for San Francisco."

"San Francisco," I repeated. It was the opposite direction I'd expected Clay to go. He had been kidnapped in Maryland, and I'd hoped he'd headed in the direction of home, even if he never actually returned.

Instead, he had fled in the opposite direction as far as the continent would allow.

If he had a passport, he could even be

in another country by now.

I couldn't get ahead of myself. If he'd left the country, there was nothing I could do. My jurisdiction on this case ended at the border. Technically, because the case wasn't on the FPA's roster, even hunting Clay down to San Francisco was beyond my authority. I'd have to pursue him on my own time.

Luckily, I had plenty of vacation and sick days built up, so Mason shouldn't be too mad if I suddenly took off work for a while.

"Is there anything else?"

Dinah tipped her head and gave me a teasing look. "I advised him to use an alias instead of his real name, if that helps."

She was joking, but that info might actually help. Even if I didn't know what name he was using, the fact that he probably wasn't going by Clay Dahler would keep me from overlooking potential leads in the future.

Having gotten what I wanted, I stood from my chair and headed for the door. "Thanks for your help. There's no need to see me out. I can find my own way."

"Don't forget our deal, Hollingsworth,"

she called after me. "I told you what you wanted to know, so don't go spreading lies about this honest business."

"Honest." I rolled my eyes. "Right."

Outside her office, the music and lights assaulted me once again. I dodged a few more wandering hands and nodded to Jerome on the way out the door. Then, I was once again back in the blissful fresh air of the outside world.

Looking back at *Dinah's Place*, I was overcome with a sense of ambivalence. A small part of me had hoped that the case of Clay Dahler would have a simple solution. That he had been under our noses all this time, working at a seedy strip club for money.

But no.

Clay Dahler was in the wind once again, and my search was going to be a lot harder than I'd hoped. I didn't have any contacts in San Francisco to rely on. I'd have to make the trip myself, and I had no idea where to start when I got there.

However, there was also a small feeling of accomplishment buried under my worry. The last time anyone had seen him for certain was almost a decade ago before he was taken. Now, I'd found someone who could confirm he was still alive just five years ago. It was an improvement, at least.

Walking away from the club, I sent a text to Sebastian about my progress, then started composing an explanation in my head to my boss to explain why I needed to suddenly run off to California on short notice.

Maybe I'd just call Roland and let him explain to his brother for me. There were perks to being best friends with the Boss's older brother.

CHAPTER FOUR

Logan

SAN FRANCISCO WAS a lot warmer than I expected. Although I had lived in Baton Rouge for four years now, and grew up in Maryland before that, I'd originally been born in New England, and the cold was still in my bones. Heat and I did not agree, and the dry heat of California was even worse. It felt like there was something missing in the air, and every breath seemed to scratch at my throat.

The smog choking the city didn't help, either.

When I arrived in the city, I'd started out by first checking in with the local police department. The detectives there were obviously overworked and not interested in helping me track down a missing person. They took a copy of the old photo I had and promised to contact me if they found anyone using the name Clay Dahler or matching his description, but I didn't hold out hope.

However, my trip to the local precinct wasn't a complete bust. One of the more sympathetic officers did give me a list of places around the city where sex workers tended to congregate. It was a place to start, at least, and would hopefully guide me to a more concrete lead.

I still held out a small hope that Clay had managed to find legitimate work somewhere. Even after my trip to *Dinah's Place*, I couldn't let go of the thought that maybe Clay had gotten lucky somewhere. Even if it was a simple job flipping burgers at McDonalds, or even something less legal like working an under the table construction job. Those options would at least be better than selling himself.

Still, I would canvas the areas on the list I'd been given and see if any of the local street workers recognized him.

Even so early in the day, people were

blatantly hooking in the back alleys. It was a shock. Baton Rouge had plenty of prostitutes as well, I'd both arrested and rescued plenty of them, but they usually didn't work so blatantly out in public during the day.

The first street I visited, I was immediately propositioned by three separate people at the same time, who then got into a squabble about who had seen me first. I barely managed to get a word in edgewise, and it took me nearly ten minutes to explain that I wasn't a potential client and what I was there for. As soon as they realized they wouldn't be getting any money from me, they immediately lost interest, barely looking at the photograph I showed them before dismissing me.

The second street I had a little more luck, because I made sure to state my intention right away before anyone could get into an argument. This time a few people took a moment to look at the photograph before shaking their head with genuine sorrow about not being able to help me.

The third location I visited was a nightmare from the get-go. The street was ruled over by an iron-fisted pimp, who was absolutely convinced that if I wasn't there as a client then I must be looking for a job. I'd had to physically restrain him to keep him from dragging me into the backdoor of a shady looking building. The photograph never even left my pocket on that trip, and I fled from the street without even uttering Clay Dahler's name.

It was the same no matter where I went. No one had any idea where Clay might be, or if he was even in the city. Granted, it was a large city, with millions of people. I probably hadn't even scratched the surface of possible places he could be, but I was still disheartened.

The sun had passed the halfway point and was on its way back toward the horizon when I stopped to rest under the covered archway of an abandoned building. Hanging my head in exhaustion, I sighed deeply.

"You having a bad day, too?"

I jumped at the sound of the unexpected voice. I hadn't even noticed the young man hiding in the shade of the archway, probably using it as cover to stay out of the midday sun.

He didn't come any closer and

remained huddled against the dirty brick wall, but he also didn't seem afraid of me as he regarded me with curiosity and concern.

"I'm looking for someone." I shrugged. "I know he came to this city a few years ago, but I don't even know if he's still here. If he is here, he might be working the streets, so I've been checking around."

The other man, who I realized was younger than I first thought, scooted a little closer so I was able to get a better look at his face. There was dirt smudged on his cheeks, and he looked thin, but there was still light in his eyes. Life hadn't broken him yet.

"I go by Jordy around here. A lot of people know me, and I know a lot of people. Maybe I can help."

Taking the picture out of my pocket for what felt like the hundredth time that day, I handed it over.

"His name is—"

"Clay."

The unexpected sound of that familiar name made me jump. "Yes. How do you..."

Before I could finish the question, Jordy shrugged and quickly handed back the photo. "I met him years ago, though he didn't look like that even back then. But the birthmark on his neck is easy to remember." He paused for a minute, regarding me with a suspicious eye, before deciding to finish his explanation. "He and I were... kept in the same place for a while."

Shit.

He'd been a victim of those damn traffickers, too. Taking a closer look at Jordy, I realized he was exactly their type. Slight stature, young looking, and blue eyes. His hair had been buzzed short so there was only about two inches left, but if it were longer, it would probably be bright blond and curly.

My immediate impulse was to sweep the young man away and take him to safety, but I couldn't even find the person I was looking for.

How was I supposed to take care of a second person as well?

"Why are you looking for him?"

Jordy's question snapped me out of my spiraling thoughts. I needed to focus. Find Clay first. Then maybe I could worry about saving other lost souls.

"His brother is looking for him, and I'm

helping in the search. I have some experience with the traffickers who took him." Jordy's eyes grew wide, and I quickly rushed to correct myself. "Not that kind of experience. I'm trying to stop them, or at least save as many victims as I can.

Jordy fell silent, obviously struggling with his thoughts.

I waited as patiently as I could, giving him the time he needed to think. He was the only lead I had found so far, and I couldn't afford to scare him away by being too pushy.

"All right," Jordy eventually declared when he'd come to some sort of decision. "Guess it can't hurt. Not like things can get much worse for guys like us. Can I borrow your phone?"

I handed it over without hesitation, and watched as he punched in a number.

Clay's lucky enough that he doesn't usually need to work the street directly. He's got a 'middleman' that anonymously sets up work for him. That's the number, but I don't know if they'll let you talk to Clay or not."

"A middleman, hmm?" I quickly saved the number in my contacts to make sure I didn't lose it. "Don't worry. I have plenty of experience dealing with 'middlemen'. I'll find some way to get through to Clay."

A plan was starting to form in my mind. It would be distasteful, but it would probably be my best bet to speak with Clay without his 'middleman' interfering.

"Hey, does Clay use an alias when he works?"

"Yeah, of course," Jordy shrugged. "We all do. Clay goes by Blue Steele. His middleman tried to convince him to go by Angel, based on his looks, but he shot that down real quick. I don't blame him. I would, too."

I gave Jordy a questioning look, and he just shrugged again. It seemed to be his go-to move whenever he was uncomfortable.

"The, um, people who took us. They called us their *little angels*. Don't think I'll be able to step inside a church again without getting flashbacks, which sucks. The family I came from was really religious. They'd be horrified to see me now."

"Don't use the word Angel. Got it. And, hey. I wouldn't be so sure about your family. They've probably been missing you and would just be happy to have you home."

This time, instead of shrugging, Jordy laughed. It was a sad, broken sound, that made me wish he would go back to shrugging.

"Kids like Clay and I weren't just taken because of our looks. It was because we were easy victims who likely wouldn't be missed. Clay's lucky in that sense. Someone misses him, but not all of us are so lucky."

What could I even say to that?

I didn't know Jordy or his situation. I couldn't guarantee that his family actually missed him, even though I was certain the traffickers had probably lied to him or at least exaggerated things in order to maintain control over the kids they took.

I clenched the phone tighter in my hand. I had to focus on Clay first. Now that I had a solid plan, I couldn't delay. If Clay got word that someone was going around the city looking for him, he might spook and run away, and then I'd never track him down again.

Still, guilt gnawed at my stomach when I left Jordy sitting under that old, abandoned archway. I gave him all the cash I had on me so he could at least get himself a decent meal and hopefully, wouldn't have to work for a few days, but that didn't ease my conscience.

I'd joined the Air Force at eighteen because I wanted to save the world, and I'd become a detective when I was twenty-two because I wanted to save people who couldn't save themselves.

The one thing that both careers had taught me, was that I couldn't save everyone, no matter how hard I tried.

CHAPTER FIVE

Clay

A GENERIC LOOKING black sedan pulled up to the side of the street. I could tell as soon as I laid eyes on it that it was a rental.

Someone didn't want to be recognized. Which meant either they were important, or they were new to these kinds of 'transactions' and were paranoid. The latter option would be fine, but if it was the former...

Well, I'd had enough experience in my life servicing 'important' men to know not to get involved with them.

Not moving from my place leaning

against the wall, I turned my attention away from the car to the rest of the back street.

I wasn't the only hooker working this street. All the regulars were out tonight. Faces I'd seen on and off for five years since coming to San Francisco. Sometimes a face would disappear, or a new one would show up, but no one ever asked any questions. It was always the same story. We didn't need to know the details.

One of the newer faces approached the car, and after talking to someone through the window for a moment, they got inside.

Hopefully they'd still be here tomorrow, but every time someone stepped into a strange car, there was always a chance that would be the last time we saw them.

The dangers of the job, and all that.

It was a slow night, and the weather wasn't looking great. Clouds had rolled across the sky, barely distinguishable from the city smog that usually blocked out the stars, but there was an electric charge in the air that said a storm was approaching.

This wasn't how I usually preferred to work. I had a better system set up with a middleman—who I refused to call my pimp—to set up appointments for me under an alias and then send me the details. The middleman got a cut, but it saved me from having to work the streets and hunt down my own jobs like this. Unfortunately, it had been a slow week, and not many jobs had come in for me. So, I'd taken to hunting down my own clients the old-fashioned way.

No matter what, I needed a client tonight. If I didn't make any money soon, then I wouldn't be able to pay my rent.

It wouldn't be the first time I'd ended up homeless. Since coming to San Francisco, I'd been kicked out of three different apartments. I always found a way to survive, but having a roof over my head was still infinitely better than sleeping on the streets.

At least it was summer right now. Homelessness in the winter sucked, even in such a warm state, but summer wasn't too bad so long as I could find shade during the day.

Tugging at my crop-top shirt, I shifted my posture on the wall to adopt a more intentional lean that showed off my figure, rather than the exhausted slump I'd been displaying before.

The work was simple. I'd done it a million times.

So why did it never get any easier?

Another car pulled onto the street. Nice, but not too nice, and not an obvious rental as the previous one had been. This one had promise. Especially when I saw that they'd disabled the light over their license plate to discreetly hide the number. This client knew what they were doing. That meant they were probably a repeat customer, and not as likely to turn out to be a serial killer.

Prostitutes talked. If street workers kept going missing after meeting with the same client, word would be spread immediately.

The car stopped closer to me, and the window rolled down. He was a portly man, but he seemed to have good hygiene at least.

Already counting the dollars in my head, I put on my best sultry look and kicked up one leg against the wall to make sure the exposed skin of my thighs was visible.

Just as I'd expected, the man called out to me.

"Hey, Angel. You free tonight?"

Angel.

The word echoed in my head, and suddenly I was no longer standing on a San Francisco street corner. I was fourteen, and I'd just woken up in a strange, locked room that would be my home for the next four years. A man I'd never seen before sat at the bottom of the bed I was lying on.

"Rise and shine, Angel."

It was an old memory that I usually kept tucked away in the back of my mind where I could pretend it didn't exist. I'd been trafficked from the age of fourteen to eighteen. There had been many bad days during that time, but the first day had been the worst.

I shook my head and dug my nails into my leg. The spark of pain helped ground me in the present and chased away the flashback. I focused my eyes once again on the man in the car who had called out to me. He was obviously upset from my lack of reaction, and I could see anger building in him. If I agreed to go with him now, I would probably be in for a rough night.

"Fuck off. I can smell that cheap

cologne from here. You couldn't afford me."

I'd learned a long time ago that men like this did not accept a gentle rejection. A firm telling off and a harsh attitude was the only answer they would respect.

The man in the car scoffed, but his anger was already fizzling out as he turned his attention to the next available body on the street.

A man so young he could still be called a boy. That one was about the same age as I was when I was kicked out of the trafficking ring for being "too old".

It was a constant paradox. Everyone standing on this street with me was simultaneously too young and too old at the same time.

Eventually, the man in the car drove away with his new purchase sitting in the passenger seat. Hopefully, the boy would manage better than I did with my first few clients on my own.

My shoulder twinged with a memory of pain. Only a week after I arrived in San Francisco, a client had twisted my arm so far behind my back that my shoulder popped out of its socket. That was when I learned the importance of choosing my own clients carefully.

Suffering through two painful flashbacks so close together had left me feeling floaty inside my head. Like I was disconnected from my body, and I imagined I was looking down on the scene and watching myself the same way I watched characters in a movie.

My character of Blue Steele shifted back into a sultry, come-hither pose and it only took him a few minutes to catch another potential client's attention. This new client had no obvious red flags—other than the fact that he was soliciting a back-alley prostitute in the first place—so Blue agreed to go with him.

I watched, completely detached from what was happening as Blue climbed into the man's car. For these few precious moments, I was no longer Clay Dahler. I was no one. Just a passive observer with no emotional attachment to what was happening.

I called this detached headspace the Midnight Zone, because I'd loved the Twilight Zone as a kid. It was my safe place outside of reality, and it had gotten me through the hardest years of my past.

Blue and the client only drove for a few

minutes before they pulled into a cheap motel. The staff at the motel were used to people bringing prostitutes there, and barely gave them a second glance. There was less than five minutes between pulling into the motel parking lot and opening the door to one of the rooms.

The decor inside was as old and tacky as every cheap motel ever made, and the bed was barely better than a block of wood as Blue was shoved down onto the mattress.

If this was a movie, I would have turned it off at this point. I couldn't turn off my life, but I could at least stop paying attention.

So, I did.

CHAPTER SIX

Clay

TWO HOURS LATER, with cash in hand and my most recent client snoring on the motel bed, I slipped into the bathroom to steal a shower. The water pressure was shit, and the provided shampoo was barely better than soap, but at least the temperature was decent.

I turned the shower to its hottest setting, letting the bathroom fill with steam until the walls were barely visible and the mirror was clouded over with moisture.

I didn't need to watch myself as I cleaned away the reminder of my latest job.

My skin was pink by the time I stepped out of the shower, and I quickly dried off before slipping back into my clothes. My blond hair was nearly long enough to touch the nape of my neck and took a while to dry. I didn't even bother to try and after ringing out as much water as possible I just tied it into a messy ponytail.

After double checking once again that the money was in my pocket, I slipped out the door without waking the man on the bed.

It was still too early for the first buses to run in this area, so I was forced to walk. I was wearing sturdy shoes, and the motel was in an area I knew so there was no chance of getting lost, but several miles was still a long distance to travel on foot when I was already tired. It had been a long night, and I just wanted to sleep, but the moth-eaten, lumpy mattress waiting for me back at my apartment wasn't exactly enticing.

The first light of dawn was just starting to show in the sky, so the shadows between streetlights didn't look so dark. It would be easy to fall into a false sense of security and think that the approaching light meant safety, but that wasn't true. In this area of the city, I would be just as likely to be mugged during the day as at night, especially since I'd just come from a job and had a few hundred dollars of cash sitting in my pocket.

I kept my eye on my surroundings, my head on a swivel, ready to run if anyone even tried to approach me. I wouldn't feel safe until I had a locked door between me and the rest of the world.

Well, *safer.* True safety was impossible.

The sun had fully risen by the time I reached my apartment, and I was once again cursing my decision to live in a place with so many steep hills.

It hadn't really been a decision. After getting away from the traffickers that had held me for four years, I took what little money I'd managed to squirrel away and bought a bus ticket for as far away as possible. My money had run out at San Francisco, and I'd never bothered to leave since then.

So, yeah, not really a decision, but I liked to think of it that way.

My hair had mostly dried in the

California heat by the time I opened the door to my apartment. I shared the space with three other roommates who I rarely saw. The apartment technically only had two bedrooms, but plywood walls had been positioned down the middle of each bedroom to turn it into four spaces. I wasn't lucky enough to get one of the spaces connected to a door, so I had to first tiptoe through my literal roommate's space until I reached my own.

On the other side of the plywood wall, there was just enough space for a mattress, a few milk crates I'd stacked into a makeshift shelf, and a clothing rack that I'd stolen from the dumpster behind a clothing store.

The shit hole cost me way more than it was worth, but it was better than being homeless, and the 'landlord' didn't ask questions so long as rent was paid on time.

Changing out of my clothes and into an old but clean pair of shorts and a T-shirt that I used for sleeping, I collapsed onto my bed. I was exhausted, but I was too twitchy to sleep. It had been a slow week before tonight, and I'd had too much time to think. Thinking meant remembering, which I didn't want to do. If there was a way to open up my brain and scoop out all my memories from my skull like it was a pint of ice scream, I'd do it in a heartbeat.

Unfortunately, such a procedure hadn't been invented yet. So, I turned to the next best thing for achieving mindlessness.

Social media.

A large crack ran through the screen of my phone, but it still worked. I could barely afford any minutes, so I only used the phone in my apartment where I had access to Wi-Fi. My fingers moved automatically as I opened a familiar Instagram.

Jason Dahler. My brother.

He still looked just the same as I remembered him. Familiar blue eyes and sandy brown hair were always the first things I noticed; similar to mine but a few shades darker. There were several images, but I focused on the one where the man was facing slightly sideways so the notch in his ear, that he'd gotten when he'd mistaken a wild bobcat for a house cat and tried to pet it, was clearly visible.

I hadn't seen Jason in person since I

was fourteen, but I'd kept up to date on his life by stalking his social media pages. I never dared to interact with anything he posted, but I looked at the pictures and made a mental note of all his milestones.

He still lived in the small Maryland town where we'd been born, had gotten married a few years ago, and owned a construction business that seemed to be doing well based on the size of his house. Of course, he may have built the house himself, too. There were bags under his eyes in his latest pictures that he'd tried to cover with makeup, but overall he seemed to be doing okay.

Every time I saw that Jason was still out there in the world, living his peaceful ordinary life, a sense of relief filled my chest.

When I'd first been released, I'd briefly considered finding my way back to Maryland. The urge to return home was so strong I was nearly choking on it. However, when I tried to picture what a homecoming would look like, I could only imagine myself as the fourteen-year-old boy I'd been before I was taken. My brother wouldn't recognize the man I was now. I wasn't the same person anymore. I was barely a person at all. Most days, I felt like a ghost walking around in a human body. Someone who died nine years ago yet kept living.

No, Jason didn't need me around. He had a happy life with a spouse, a respectable job, and a nice house with a white picket fence. That wasn't even a metaphor. I could literally see the white picket fence around his house in some of his pictures.

Everything in Jason's life was so proper and clean, two words which didn't describe me. For all I knew, he'd probably forgotten about me. I was likely just a passing thought that entered his brain every now and then before disappearing just as quickly as it came.

I told myself over and over that I was staying away for his sake, but that was a lie. The real reason I'd put myself on the opposite side of the country from him was fear.

What if I did go back, and he rejected me?

That would hurt worse than anything a client had done to me in the past. I'd survived a lot of pain, but I wasn't strong enough to survive Jason's rejection.

Turning off my screen, the pictures of Jason's life were replaced with my own reflection. The crack in the screen cut right across my face, scattering my image into fractured pieces.

I snorted in disgust.

Why was I being so maudlin today?

Nothing had changed. Today had been the same as yesterday and would be the same as tomorrow. There was no reason for me to be more upset now than any other time. This was my life, and I would just have to keep living it until someday I died.

End of story.

Shoving my phone under my pillow, I threw myself down on the bed and shut my eyes, determined to get at least a few hours of sleep before one of my roommates inevitably woke me up.

It seemed as though I had barely closed my eyes before I was startled awake by a loud noise.

"What the hell?"

My brain wasn't fully awake, so it took a moment for me to realize what I was seeing.

There was someone in my room, riffling through my stuff. In their hurry they'd knocked over one of the milk crates I used as furniture, which had woken me up.

It was one of my roommates. For a moment, I wondered what they were doing here, and my brain supplied only innocent reasons, still half lost in a mix of dreams and memories.

Then I noticed the wad of cash in their hand, rumpled green bills practically being crushed within their grip, and dazed confusion immediately snapped into anger.

"What the hell are you doing?"

Asking was pointless. I knew what they were doing, but the words still tumbled out of my mouth even as I shoved the man away from my stuff.

Unfortunately, my roommate had at least fifty pounds and several inches on me. My shove didn't move him more than a few inches. I tried to snatch my money out of his hand, but he just shoved me away, so I landed back on my mattress.

"I had a bad night at the poker tables," my roommate said as he shoved my money in his pocket. "It'll just be a loan. I'll pay you back."

"The fuck you will."

My blood boiled in my veins, tightening my throat while spurring my muscles into movement at the same time. I acted on instinct and swung at him, miraculously managing to land a hit square on his jaw. This time he staggered back and fell against the plywood that divided the room. Something cracked, and while it was probably just the old wood breaking under his weight, a sadistic part of me hoped it was his jaw.

"You fucking creep," I shouted as I gathered up the bills that hadn't made it into his pocket yet. "I'm not paying for your gambling addiction."

I'd managed to hit him pretty hard, and a bruise was already forming on his jaw, but that didn't keep him down for long. Based on his blown pupils, he was probably on something, because he didn't seem to feel any pain. He sent the plywood divider crashing to the floor in pieces as he suddenly surged forward.

His fist hit me square in the face so fast I didn't even see it move. The whole left side of my face exploded in pain, and I doubled over. Another punch hit me in the stomach, which sent me to my knees, then a kick to the ribs put me on the ground.

I curled into a ball on my mattress in a desperate attempt to protect myself from any further blows, but thankfully my roommate seemed satisfied now that I wasn't fighting back.

"Stupid fucking whore," the man muttered as he moved around the room. "Just go fuck someone else if you need money so bad."

He kicked the remains of the plywood divider on his way out, then slammed the door behind him.

I lay on my mattress, barely moving for several minutes as I clutched my throbbing face. At first, I was too afraid to really probe the wound, scared that he had broken something. As my shock faded, I was able to determine that the area around my eye was swollen, but my nose didn't hurt too much and there didn't seem to be any blood.

My ribs and stomach also ached, but I could breathe without pain, so I didn't think anything was broken there either.

I would have a nasty black eye and several other bruises, but at least I wouldn't have to go to the hospital.

In the silence of the room, the sudden

ringing of my phone was like an ice pick to my ears. I uncurled from my defensive ball just enough to fish the device out from under my pillow.

"What?"

An auto-generated voice answered me with only five words.

"Blue Steele, you have a client."

Then the phone clicked off, immediately followed by the ping of an incoming text message that would provide the client's info.

This was how I usually got my clients, and on a different day I would have been glad for a job I didn't have to go hunt down myself.

But, fuck, I really wasn't up to another job right now. I felt like I would fall apart if I moved too quickly, and the thought of handing myself over for someone else's use turned my stomach even more than normal.

My gaze wandered to my hand, and the single twenty-dollar bill clutched in my grip. It was all that I'd managed to save from my roommates pilfering. If I didn't make more soon, then never mind affording rent. I wouldn't even be able to eat.

Dragging myself to my feet, I checked the info for the client. I had two hours before I needed to arrive at the specified hotel.

The address was one of the nicer hotels in the area. Not too fancy, but expensive enough that I'd only met clients there a few times, and each time I'd managed to make a pretty penny for my efforts.

That thought brought me a little energy. With any luck, the client wouldn't be too demanding, and I could end the day with more money than I'd started with.

Leaving my half-destroyed room behind, I headed for the apartment's singular bathroom so I could clean up and get ready. A cold washcloth would hopefully reduce some of the swelling around my eye, but there would be no hiding the bruise. Couldn't afford the makeup needed for such a coverup.

Hopefully the client wouldn't demand a discount for damaged goods.

CHAPTER SEVEN

Logan

SITTING IN THE hotel room, waiting for the prostitute I'd hired to show up, reminded me of my brief time working undercover on a case against one of the Mexican Cartels.

Back then, I'd been lucky enough to keep my hands clean while maintaining my cover, but I swore I'd never put myself in that position again. Yet, here I was, once again pretending to be a scumbag for the sake of the "greater" good.

Somehow, it felt even worse this time. Before, I'd agreed to the mission without understanding what it would really cost me, emotionally. This time, I knew exactly what it meant, yet I did it anyway.

Reminding myself that I wasn't actually going to sleep with Clay didn't help. I'd hired him, and as far as he knew I was just another client. It made me feel dirty. Unfortunately, the number for his "middleman" was the only lead I had, and the only way I would get close to him was as a client.

At least the hotel would give us privacy. I'd even gotten there early to check the room for hidden cameras, just to be sure.

Twenty minutes passed as I sat on a hard-backed chair, one of the room's only pieces of furniture that wasn't the bed, fighting a war with myself. I lost track of time, and when someone knocked on the door, I jumped.

Show time. The next few minutes would determine whether my mission succeeded or failed.

As I reached for the door handle, a thought struck me.

What if it wasn't Clay waiting on the other side?

I only had Jordy's word that Blue Steele was Clay's working alias. Maybe he'd lied, or maybe Clay had passed the name on to someone else by now.

It was too late to turn back. I was already opening the door; I would simply have to face whatever greeted me on the other side.

"I've got a delivery for Mike Smith," the man standing on the other side of the door said.

It was a code phrase meant to make sure I was the right client, but I barely heard him. I barely even remembered to reply.

"Oh, um. Yeah. Hold on. I left the money in my other jacket. Come in while I get it."

I stuttered my way through the correct coded response, too busy looking at his neck. The man wore a long coat that covered most of his body, but most of his neck was still visible, revealing the seahorse shaped birthmark there.

Unless I was unlucky enough to come across another prostitute with the exact same birthmark, this was Clay Dahler.

"Sooo," Clay drawled, obviously sounding uncomfortable. "Can I come in?"

"Oh, right. Yeah."

Stupid.

I was already messing it up. Any normal client would have ushered him out of the hall, and away from prying eyes immediately, but I'd just been standing there overcome with a sense of nervous relief. I felt more like a shy teenager about to ask his crush to prom, rather than an experienced investigator undertaking a mission.

As I stepped out of the way of the door, I finally looked up from his neck and I had to withhold my gasp.

The picture I'd been given of Clay was over a decade old, but I'd never really thought about what that meant. In my mind he was still that smiling, wide-eyed child. While there were still enough similarities to let me know I had the same person, Clay had outgrown his childish features. Instead of a fluttering little cupid from a Renaissance painting, he looked like the *Genie du Maal* come to life.

The history of the statue says that the Cathedral of Saint Paul had hired Joseph Geefs to create an image of Lucifer, but the final product was deemed so beautiful it distracted the church's parishioners. So, they'd commissioned Joseph Geefs brother, Guillaume, to remake the statue.

Yet, the new statue turned out more beautiful than the first, and the church was presented with an even greater distraction on their hands.

As Clay walked past me, I could understand the church's distress.

A man like this could tempt anyone into sin.

Wavy blond hair fell to his shoulders, showing off the line of his neck. His blue eyes were no longer round with youth, but instead were sharp and sultry. He was lean, yet still soft, and moved with the grace of a dancer. The long coat he wore did its best to hide his body, but nothing could disguise the length of his legs.

The only blemish was the painfully dark bruise marring his left eye. Some makeup had been applied to try and hide it, but not enough. The bruise was obviously still fresh, and slightly swollen around the edges.

Once Clay was inside, I closed the door and kept my back turned toward the room as I took a deep breath. Getting angry over the bruise wouldn't do any good, and there was no reason for me to notice his looks. Beautiful or ugly, healthy or injured, he was a victim in need of rescue. End of story.

"So, is this your first time?" Clay called from behind me.

I turned around, intending to correct him, but my words died in my throat.

In the thirty seconds I'd taken to regain my composure, Clay had stripped off his coat and draped himself across the hotel bed in a provocative pose.

The long coat made sense, now. He never would have made it through the hotel lobby without getting harassed in an outfit like that. His shirt was more jewelry than cloth, and his black shorts clung to every curve and crease of his body.

Something hot throbbed deep inside me. At first, I didn't understand what I was feeling, and I stood in the center of the room, frozen with indecision.

Whatever expression I was making must not have been pleasant, for Clay put on an over-exaggerated pout and shifted so that his legs rubbed together.

"Don't be mad. There's nothing to be embarrassed about. It's obvious that this is your first time hiring someone. I can teach you a few things, if you like."

He obviously meant it as an invitation, and even let his legs fall open a little.

The throbbing came again, and I finally realized what I felt.

I was aroused.

Disgust immediately washed through me, and I nearly stumbled away from the bed. Only by gripping onto the arm of the nearby chair was I able to stay standing.

"I'm not..." My stomach roiled and I had to stop speaking for fear that I would throw up. I'd never hated myself more than I did in that moment.

How could I possibly be feeling any sort of desire?

I'd seen beautiful people before. I'd even been propositioned before. It had never affected me. Yet, the sight of Clay splayed out on the bed, enticing me over with both his looks and his words, was almost more than I could take.

I bit the inside of my cheek until I tasted blood, and the pain brought some clarity back to my hormone-soaked brain.

Clay wasn't here by choice. He was only here because I'd literally purchased him.

Clearing my throat, I tried speaking again. "I'm not interested in that."

"Oh." Clay closed his legs and sat up a little straighter on the bed, but the inviting look in his eyes never left. "My standard rate only includes oral, and sex in the missionary position or doggy style. If you want something more than that, you'll have to pay more. Upfront. And I won't do anything that leaves permanent marks."

The images his words brought to mind left me stunned, speechless.

No.

Focus.

I was here for a purpose.

Shaking away my inappropriate thoughts, I forced myself to speak.

"No, I mean, I'm not here for any of... that." I waved vaguely in his direction and the bed, trying to summarize everything I couldn't bear to say in one gesture.

I'd planned a dozen different ways to explain things in my head while I'd been looking for him, but now that I was faced with the man in question, I forgot every single one of them. It probably wouldn't have mattered anyway. I'd planned my explanations as if talking to a scared child. The man in front of me, sharpened by the harsh realities of the world, wouldn't have responded well to such a patronizing tone.

Instead, I went for a straightforward approach.

"I'm here because your brother is looking for you."

Suspicion darkened Clay's blue eyes, so they looked almost black in the hotel's cheap lighting. He sat up fully on the bed and tugged at his clothes as if to pull them closer around his body, but there wasn't enough material. Instead, he just grabbed empty air as he wrapped his arms around himself.

"What are you talking about? I don't have a brother."

"Jason Dahler."

Clay flinched at the sound of his brother's name.

"I don't—"

I cut him off before he could try to lie to me again. "You're Clay Dahler, right? Your brother, Jason, hired a private investigator to find you." Approaching the bed on slow, careful steps, I held out both my hands, so they remained in sight at all times. "I'm sorry I hired you under false pretenses like this, but all I could find was a phone number, and this seemed like the only way I'd be able to talk to you."

I was still several steps away when Clay stood quickly from the bed, giving me a wide berth so he always remained outside of arms reach.

"You have the wrong person. I don't have a brother, and no one's looking for me. Sorry. You came all this way for nothing. I'll try to get you your money back, so, let's both just leave, and we can forget this ever happened."

"I don't have the wrong person." Fishing the photo out of my pocket, I held it up for him to see. "This is the last picture your brother has of you. After so much time, there haven't been many leads to find you, but he hasn't given up."

Clay barely glanced at the picture before looking away. "That isn't me. I'm sorry."

He started heading for the door, still keeping as far away from me as the hotel's walls would allow. If he managed to leave, I'd have a hard time tracking him down again.

In a moment of panic, I grabbed his wrist and pulled him away from the door. "Wait. Please. Just hear me out."

My desperate words had barely left my mouth when a sudden pain snapped my head to the side. The room spun for a moment, and when I regained my senses, Clay was gone.

On the other side of the room, the open door swung slightly back and forth on its stiff hinges.

As the dizziness faded, I rubbed my jaw and flinched at the new bruise I found there.

He'd punched me. It was a shock, but not unexpected.

What had I been thinking, grabbing him like that?

Of course he lashed out. If I'd ever acted like that with one of the victims who came to the FPA office back in Baton Rouge, I'd have been fired immediately. My only excuse was that panic had made me stupid.

So, so stupid.

I was half inclined to punch myself again, just for good measure. I'd certainly deserve it.

As I stood in the middle of the room, chastising myself and wondering what I was going to do now, I noticed something on the floor.

Clay had been in such a hurry to get away from me, he'd left his coat behind.

The heavy fabric lay draped over the back of the room's only chair, swaying in the breeze from the air-conditioning.

With numb fingers, I picked up the coat. It felt too heavy, even taking the thick fabric into account. Checking each of the pockets, I pulled out a wallet. The thing was so frayed and stained, Clay had probably found it in a dumpster somewhere, but the zipper still worked to hold the whole thing closed.

There wasn't much inside. A few wrinkled bills that didn't add up to more than thirty dollars, several condoms, a coupon for frozen yogurt, and a library card.

It wasn't much, but it was enough. A library card required an address. I could use it to find where he lived.

I'd already pulled out my phone and was searching through my contacts when I stopped and thought about what I was doing.

I'd found him. Technically, that was all Jason had hired *Alias Investigations* to do, and I technically wasn't even a private investigator. I had no authority to go hunting down a civilian and violating his privacy. I'd found Clay, I'd spoken to him, and he'd made his choice to leave.

Did I have the right to ignore that choice and keep pursuing him anyway?

Slumping down onto the edge of the bed, I braced my elbows on my knees and hung my head as I dialed a different number on my phone.

"Hey, Logan," Sebastian's voice greeted me. "You find anything?"

"Yep. I found Clay Dahler. But now I've got a bigger problem."

As quickly and accurately as possible, I explained everything that had happened so far, including the sheer luck that had led me to finding Clay in the first place, and the way I'd practically chased him out of the room in my panic when I realized he was leaving.

Sebastian told me off for the last part, though he didn't say anything I hadn't already said to myself. Overall, however, he wasn't as disappointed as I expected.

"We knew this wouldn't be easy," he reminded me though the phone. "It's a miracle you've gotten as far as you have. I certainly wouldn't have known about *Dinah's Place*, and even if I had, she wouldn't have told me anything. That's all thanks to you. Now that we know he's in the city, we just need to decide what to do next."

The phone was on speaker mode, sitting on the bed next to me. This left my hands free to turn the library card over and over.

"I know what to do next. I'm just not sure if I should. I mean, if Clay doesn't want to see his brother again, it's not my place to force him."

The phone fell silent for a while, and I checked to make sure the call was still connected. The timer was still running, indicating the call was still going, but Sebastian wasn't saying anything.

"If I don't pursue him, I'm always going to regret it," I admitted in a very small voice. "It's a horrible, selfish reason. My regrets shouldn't matter, but I'm not sure how to live with myself otherwise."

Faint whispering could be heard from Sebastian's side of the call. He seemed to be talking to someone else, though I couldn't hear what they were saying. I waited while Sebastian finished his other conversation, and then his voice rang loud and clear.

"Clay never said he didn't want to see his brother. He claimed he didn't have one. That doesn't sound like he's made a choice. That sounds like denial. He's probably survived all this time by locking away his painful thoughts and memories, so he didn't have to face them. Reminding him of his brother is breaking down those defenses. I'd say you should go after him. Try one more time. If he makes a clear decision and says he wants nothing to do with his brother, then respect that, but give him the chance to make that decision."

Sighing, I ran my hand through my hair, which dragged my carefully styled bangs into my face. "Even if I did find him again, what's to stop him from reacting the same way as he did this time? He's probably even more scared of me now."

"I might have an idea for that. Just focus on finding Clay for now. I'll try to come up with a better way for you to get through to him."

CHAPTER EIGHT

Logan

TWO PHONE CALLS.

That was all it took to find Clay's address.

The benefits of knowing the right people.

Less than twelve hours after our disastrous first meeting in the hotel, I stood outside Clay's apartment building, staring up at the floor where I knew he lived.

I'd already been there for fifteen minutes, and my feet felt rooted to the sidewalk.

If I waited any longer, I may as well

just give up and leave. Standing there in indecision wasn't doing anyone any good.

Taking a deep breath, I approached the building. The front door was locked, and required someone from inside to buzz me through. There wasn't a doorman or anyone I could reason with, so I fell back on the tried-and-true method of pushing all the call buttons at the same time. In a building this big, someone was always expecting a delivery or a guest. I only had to hit each button twice before getting the telltale click of the door unlocking.

Clay's address was on the twelfth floor, right in the center of the building. In my years working for the FPA and as a detective in Maryland, I'd been to a lot of decrepit places, and this building was right up there with the worst of them. It had obviously been written off as a lost cause by the health department years ago, and I doubted a safety inspection had been done in the last decade. It was a miracle the place hadn't been condemned already, but someone must have been making money off the people living there in order to keep it around.

Based on the sounds I could hear through the paper-thin walls, there were almost as many humans as rats who called the building home, way over the legal occupancy limit.

There was no elevator, so I had to climb up to the twelfth floor. The staircase was the worst part of the building, filled with dirt and rubbish, and suspicious red stains on the walls that I tried not to think about.

I didn't even dare breathe through my nose. The building also had no air-conditioning, and the San Francisco heat made everything smell ten times worse.

Despite being in good shape and regularly hitting the gym, I was panting by the time I reached the twelfth floor. If Clay had to climb these stairs every day, he must have the legs of an Olympic athlete.

The door to Clay's apartment was barely hanging on its hinges. There wasn't even a point in knocking. I could have forced my way in just by breathing too hard on the door, but I knocked anyway for the sake of politeness. Though I rapped my knuckles against the doorframe, rather than the door itself.

Almost immediately, the door flew open.

"What?"

I stared at the unknown man for a moment, trying to figure out what to say. The man, who I hoped was Clay's roommate, was obviously high off his ass. He swayed where he stood, clinging to the doorframe for support, and couldn't fully focus on me.

"I'm looking for Clay Dahler."

"Who?"

Just in case Clay's roommate didn't know about his job, I didn't dare call him Blue Steele. Instead, I gave a detailed description of Clay.

"Oh, him." The man pointed over his shoulder, nearly losing his balance in the process. "Yeah, over there."

Then he wandered away from the door, as if completely forgetting I existed.

It wasn't exactly an invitation to come in, but I'd take what I could get.

The door to Clay's room was no better than the front door and gave little resistance as I pushed it open.

The room inside was small, made even smaller by a piece of plywood dividing it in half. At some point the plywood had been broken and patched back together with duct tape, so it stood in a jagged zigzag rather than a straight line. One side of the plywood was stuffed to the gills with junk. Old lawn chairs, pizza boxes, broken lamps, and even a collection of car parts were all tangled together. It looked more like a dumping ground than a place where someone actually lived.

The other side of the plywood was drastically sparse in comparison, holding only a mattress, a clothing rack, and a couple of crates. It was also blessedly occupied. Clay's familiar figure sat on the mattress, curled into a ball with his arms around his knees as he leaned against the wall.

I couldn't tell if he was asleep or not, so I knocked on the wall near the door to get his attention.

"Clay?"

Clay's head shot up and he stared at me with wide, frantic eyes.

"What the hell?"

I barely had time to duck as he chucked something at my head. It flew by too fast for me to see what it was but based on the crashing sound I heard when it hit the wall, it wasn't something I wanted making contact with my skull.

"Clay, wait."

"I can't believe you, bastard," Clay screeched as he threw something else at me. "You actually followed me. Fuck off and get out!"

I ducked again and this time I stayed down in a crouched position, hoping it would make me seem less threatening.

"Clay, please. If you want me to leave, I'll leave. But just hear me out first."

"Why should I?"

He'd run out of things to throw at me and seemed to be contemplating whether he'd be able to pick up the clothing rack and wield it as a weapon.

"I'll pay you."

I'd blurted out the words before I could actually think about what I was saying, and I immediately wanted to slap myself. Yet, surprisingly, it was enough for Clay to calm down and stop plotting how to bash my brain in.

"What do you mean?"

It was the best response I'd gotten so far, so I rolled with it. "I'll pay you for your time, and I won't come near you, if you'll just listen for a few minutes. All right?"

Clay eyed me up and down, and I noticed the side of his mouth twitch like he was trying not to smile. I probably looked ridiculous, sweaty and disheveled from my climb up the stairs, and crouched awkwardly on the floor like I was hiding from an incoming missile.

"How much?"

Quickly searching my wallet, I pulled out all the bills I had.

"A hundred bucks."

I could see the wheels turning in his head as he eyed the cash.

Eventually making a decision, he kicked one of the milk crates over to me.

"Put the money in there, then slide it back over. And you stay on that side of the room. If you take one step toward me, we're done."

Following his orders, I handed over the money without moving my feet so much as an inch. I also stayed crouched. It was an uncomfortable position, but it seemed to help Clay feel more comfortable in my presence.

As soon as he had the cash in hand, he quickly counted the bills then stashed them under his pillow. The action reminded me of a squirrel burying nuts for winter, which shouldn't have been as endearing as it was. If I'd had any more money on me, I would have handed it over just to watch him hide it again.

"Okay," he said, once the money was secure. "You've bought my time. Now talk."

Shaking my head, I pulled out my phone. "I don't need to talk. I just need you to listen to something."

I set the phone in the middle of the floor, as far as I could reach without moving my feet, and hit play on the video that was already cued up.

"Hey, Clay. Long time no see. Heh. That sounds too casual, doesn't it, but what do you even say in a situation like this?"

Clay's reaction to the sound of his brother's voice was as dramatic as it was instantaneous. He drew back from the phone like it would explode until his back was plastered to the wall.

"It's a recording," I assured him as I hit pause on the video. "I figured a live video call would be too much, but hopefully, this can help prove that your brother really did hire me."

Well, he hired the Roth brothers, who then asked for my help, but Clay didn't need to know those details.

Slowly, Clay pulled away from the wall and reached toward the phone with trembling hands. I didn't move a muscle, I barely even breathed, as he held my phone up closer to his face and started the video again.

"*What do you even say in a situation like this? 'I miss you' doesn't cut it. Sometimes I wonder if I even remember you accurately. After so long, you feel more like an imaginary friend I once had, rather than a brother. I keep all your old stuff in a box in the attic, just to prove to myself that you're real. That you might come home someday.*"

I stopped listening and tried to block out the words coming from the video. It had been Sebastian's idea for Jason to record something, and I was ashamed that I hadn't thought of it myself. Ever since I'd received the video, I'd been dying of curiosity about what it contained, but I hadn't watched it. The message on that video wasn't for me, and that hadn't changed even now that I was in the same room. I considered stepping out, but I was too afraid to leave Clay alone in case he ran away again. So, instead, I turned away to face the broken plywood divider and hummed to myself.

Yet, despite my efforts, I couldn't help

overhearing some parts of the video.

"The private investigators I hired won't tell me what happened to you, but I've done my own research. There's only so many reasons for a kid to suddenly go missing like that."

I started humming louder and bit the inside of my cheek against the shame I felt intruding on a private moment like this.

While I hadn't watched the video, I'd seen the timestamp and knew it was about ten minutes long. We were coming up toward the end of the video when a new sound caught my attention. A soft, wet sniffing sound came from behind me. It was so quiet that at first, I thought it was a part of the video. Looking over my shoulder, I saw Clay sitting in the middle of his mattress, phone clutched tightly in his hands only a few inches from his face, and tears quietly streaming from both eyes.

"I don't care what the truth is. I don't care what you have or haven't been through. I don't even care if you never come home or even want to see me again. All I want... all I want is to know that you're safe. That you're out there

somewhere, living a good life."

Clay gasped and bit his lip, trembling from head to toe. The phone slipped from his fingers onto the mattress as heaving sobs wracked his chest. He curled up and cried into his knees, creating a perfect ball of misery.

I didn't dare stand up for fear of startling him more. So, I stayed crouched on the floor, awkwardly Spiderman-walking my way over to him. As gently as I could, I put a hand on his shoulder.

As soon as I touched him, his body reacted like it was spring-loaded. Except, instead of moving away from me like I expected, he pounced closer and buried his face against my shoulder. I held him as he cried, feeling his tears soaking through my shirt as I stroked his hair. While he no longer looked like the child he'd once been, in that moment, he still felt like that scared little boy.

"I won't tell you that it's going to be okay, because I can't guarantee something like that, and you probably wouldn't believe me anyway. But I promise that your brother is telling the truth. All he wants is for you to be safe and happy, whether that means returning to your old home, or finding a new one somewhere else. Whatever you want."

After a few minutes, Clay's sobbing calmed down enough for him to speak, though his tears never fully stopped.

"I-I want... to go home."

"All right." I squeezed his shoulder in what I hoped was a comforting gesture. "If that's your wish, then it'll be done."

"No, not all right." He shoved me away, though not very hard. It was more of a dismissive gesture than an actual attempt to make me leave. "How am I supposed to get there?"

Grabbing the cash that I'd given him out from under his pillow, he threw the wadded-up bills at me. "A hundred bucks isn't gonna cover it. Even a bus ticket would be more than that. It doesn't matter if I want to leave. I can't. I'm stuck here."

Gathering up the discarded bills, I smoothed out the wrinkles from the paper and placed them back into his hand. "Don't worry about the money. I'll take you there."

His tears finally stopped though their ghosts still left tracks down his cheeks, and he looked at the bills in confusion.

"What? You'll... but Jason lives in Maryland. That's all the way on the other side of the country."

"Do you have any ID?"

Clay shook his head, staring at me like I was some strange creature in a zoo.

He could stare all he wanted. I was too busy making plans. "Without ID a plane ticket is out of the question. But I have a car, so long as you don't mind a bit of a long car ride."

His blue eyes were wide and glittered with his recent tears. The genuine confusion on his face made him look much younger than the sultry vixen that first showed up at the hotel. It reminded me that, despite everything he'd been through, he was only twenty-three.

"I can pay you." He offered up his fist of bills.

Shaking my head, I closed his fingers tighter around the bills and pushed them toward him.

"No need. Your brother already hired me."

Or, close enough. Jason Dahler had paid *Alias Investigations*, but I wasn't seeing a dollar of that money. Nor did I intend to ask for any payment. This was a personal mission.

Clay wiped the remains of tears from his face, and some of the sharp intelligence returned to his eyes. "My brother paid you to find me. I doubt that included a personal escort. What do you want?"

Looking directly into his eyes, I answered as sincerely as I could. "I want to take you home."

Only once I heard my own words did I realize the double meaning and hurried to correct myself. "Your home. I want to take you to *your* home." As I stuttered through my explanation, I waved my hands in front of me as if that could fend off any misunderstanding. "In Maryland. Where your brother is waiting. Nothing more."

Clay still didn't look convinced, but he also didn't seem to be afraid of me anymore, so I considered it progress.

"Fine," he finally said. "Give me some time to pack up, and we can leave." We both looked around the small space that barely counted as half a bedroom.

For the first time since meeting him, Clay looked embarrassed, and a blush turned his cheeks a fetching shade of pink.

"Well, you probably won't need to wait very long."

I patted him on the shoulder, but quickly drew my hand back when he shied away from my touch.

"Take as long as you need. I have to make a phone call anyway."

As Clay started packing his meager belongings, which would probably fit into a single trash bag, I retrieved my phone from the floor and stepped out of the apartment into the building's hallway.

The phone rang several times, nearly switching over to voicemail, before it was finally picked up.

"Logan, you asshole."

I leaned against the brown-stained wall and took comfort in my friend and fellow detective's familiar voice. "Hello to you, too, Roland. Why am I an asshole this time?"

"You never take personal time. Even when you got shot by that trigger-happy pimp, you wouldn't use your vacation days. Then you suddenly leave without warning and don't even tell me where you were going, and I've got to take over your unfinished work."

I laughed, certain that even if he

couldn't see me, he would know I meant it in a friendly way. "Don't give me that crap. I just wrapped up my most recent case, so there shouldn't be much work for you to take over."

I could hear him pouting through the silence. "Fine. What's up? Why are you calling? Something wrong with your 'vacation'?"

"Well... I need you to talk to your brother for me."

The tone of his silence changed, and now I knew he was scowling. "Depends if you need me to talk to him as my brother, or as our Boss."

"Whichever option will let me take more time off without repercussions."

His sigh was so loud, I could almost feel his breath through the phone. "Fine. If it was anyone else, I'd say no. But it's you. You wouldn't ask if it wasn't important. How long do you need?"

"At least a week." I pictured a general map of the road we'd have to take to get from California to Maryland, and the distance we'd have to travel. "Actually, probably more like two weeks."

"And are you going to tell me what's so important that you have to disappear for two weeks?”

"Sorry. Can't say." I looked back at the door to the apartment where Clay was packing inside. "But, trust me. It'll be life changing."

CHAPTER NINE

Clay

THE CALIFORNIA LANDSCAPE rolled past the window, sunny and bright like it had been snatched right off a postcard. I sat in the passenger seat in the car, pretending to watch the scenery when I was actually using the reflection in the window to study the man in the driver's seat next to me.

His dark hair was pushed back into a windswept style that probably took a lot more effort to create than it looked. He had a healthy tan complexion that seemed to be a mix of regular sun exposure and natural coloration. Even when his face was neutral, his expression emanated warm friendliness, like he'd never known anything but happiness in his life. This was only emphasized by his light brown eyes that glinted with specks of gold in the sunlight.

He'd introduced himself as Logan Hollingsworth.

It was a mouthful of a name for a seemingly straightforward man. He'd promised to take me to Maryland so I could reunite with my brother, and that seemed to be exactly what he was doing.

I didn't trust it.

People didn't give away so much as five dollars without an ulterior motive. There was no way this man was going to drive me all the way from one side of the country to the other without getting something out of it.

So why had I gone with him so easily?

A few kind words and I'd eagerly piled my entire life into his car. I was usually much more careful, but somehow this man had gotten past my defenses and convinced me to come with him before I even realized what I was agreeing to.

Well, I questioned why I trusted him, but I already knew the answer. I'd come with him because I wanted his promises to be true. I was so homesick and eager to reunite with Jason that I was willing to delude myself into trusting a stranger.

When I ended up murdered and buried in a ditch somewhere, I'd have nothing to blame but my own desperation.

Hopefully, it wouldn't be that bad. So long as I lived to the end of this road trip and actually got to see my brother again, I'd consider it worthwhile.

"You can put some music on, if you like." Logan's voice interrupted my thoughts.

I met his eye in the window's reflection and found him smiling at me.

Did he realize I'd been watching him the whole time?

"It's fine. I don't really care about music."

Logan didn't argue. He just shrugged and turned on the radio to some local station playing a mix of different popular genera.

Now that we had music for a distraction, I thought he would fall silent so we could continue ignoring each other, but he was apparently determined to strike up a conversation.

"You know, I grew up in Maryland, too. You're originally from Kent Island, right? I'm from Saint Michaels."

I gave him a noncommittal noise to maintain the bare minimum of politeness. "So, you're from right across the bay."

"Yep. I haven't been back to the state in a few years, but I've still got some friends there that I keep in contact with. Did you hear about the ship that blew up off the coast of Baltimore not too long ago?"

My eyes flickered over toward him for a moment, but quickly returned to the window. "I didn't hear about that."

"Huh, yeah." His head bobbed as he tapped the steering wheel in time to the music. "The official report was that the ship experienced some sort of malfunction, but there are rumors that there was Mafia activity going on."

Was that supposed to be a warning, or was this just an attempt at small talk?

The fact that I couldn't tell the difference probably said more about me than it did about him.

I didn't respond, and just nodded vaguely to everything that he said. Eventually, he gave up the one-sided conversation and we sat in silence, with only the radio and the sound of the road passing by to fill the air between us.

When Logan had been talking, I'd wanted him to shut up, but now that he had, I realized I actually preferred the sound of his voice. Without his words to distract me, there was too much extra space in my head. My thoughts ran wild with possibilities, showing me images of all the ways this could end badly for me.

I could end up dead in a ditch somewhere.

Or maybe this whole thing had been a lie, and I'd get to Maryland only to find that my brother wanted nothing to do with me after all.

Or maybe, Logan's "nice guy" persona was just an act meant to lure me in. He was a stranger to me. For all I knew, he could be the same as the people who kidnapped me when I was a kid and he was intending to sell me just like they had.

I'd already left that particular version of hell behind. I would rather die than go back.

My heart rate sped up, and my breathing turned shallow until I was on the verge of a panic attack.

No.

I couldn't panic now.

If Logan was sincere, then he might decide I was too much trouble to bother with. If he was lying, then panicking would only make it easier for him to take advantage of me.

My vision turned fuzzy around the edges, and I felt myself falling into the Midnight Zone. That detached headspace always helped me get though difficult events, and it would help me this time as well.

I imagined I was floating a few feet above the car, pulled along like a kite on a string. My body—that of Blue Steele—was still trapped in the car, but I, Clay Dahler, could surf the winds and admire the landscape all I wanted without any disturbances. From this vantage point, I could see much farther into the horizon. If I squinted and focused real hard, I could even see the ocean.

I recalled a moment when I was younger, and I'd heard the original version of *The Little Mermaid* for the first time. I'd cried when the mermaid had turned into sea foam. Now, however, that outcome didn't seem too bad.

Sea foam had no feelings. No worries. It remembered nothing and was free to ride the crest of the ocean waves forever, undisturbed.

Yeah. That sounded like a pretty good fate after all.

The car eventually came to a stop, but it wasn't until a hand shook my shoulder that I snapped out of the Midnight Zone and back into my own body.

Blinking several times to clear the haze from my vision, I scowled over at Logan and shrugged his hand off my shoulder.

"What is it?"

"We're stopping for lunch. Come on." He nodded toward the roadside diner sitting right in front of us.

"All right. I'll just wait here." I leaned my head against the window, ready to take a nap in the noonday sun streaming through the glass. Visiting the Midnight Zone always left me feeling tired afterward, like I'd run a mental marathon.

However, before I could close my eyes, Logan nudged my shoulder again.

"What? I'm not leaving you out here. Come on. We've already been on the road for several hours. You must be hungry by now."

As subtly as I could, I checked the clock on the car's radio. Yep. Four hours had passed since we started driving.

I had no concept of time when I was lost in the Midnight Zone. It could have been minutes or hours for all I knew. In the past, when I was still being held captive, my trips to the Midnight Zone could even last for days.

Food sounded great right now, especially since I hadn't eaten since yesterday, but there was just one problem.

"Can't afford it. I'll grab something from a vending machine later."

Without saying anything, Logan exited the car and closed the door behind him. I thought that was the last of it and settled back against the window for my nap, but a moment later my own door opened, and I nearly tumbled onto the concrete.

Logan caught me, strong hands barely struggling to support my weight.

"I promised to get you to Maryland," he said, letting me go as soon as he knew I was stable. "That includes food. I'm not letting you starve for the whole trip."

The feeling of his hands on me

unnerved me. I was used to people grabbing me for all kinds of reasons, but I couldn't remember the last time someone had supported me. When I fell, I either caught myself or hit the ground. There was never another option.

"All right." I grabbed my bag from the backseat—not willing to go anywhere without my stuff just in case I ended up stranded—and stepped out of the car. "But you might want to rethink that offer. I'll eat you out of house and home if given the chance."

He just laughed as he closed the car door behind me. "I'll take my chances."

The diner was just like the kind you'd see in a cliché road trip movie from the fifties, right down to the black and white checkerboard floor and red vinyl seats. I didn't even think they still made restaurants like this, but the business seemed to be leaning into the aesthetic. Even the food on the menu had been given fifties-themed names.

I wasn't sure how long Logan's promise to pay for me would last, so when the waiter came, I took advantage while I could. Logan said nothing, but I watched his eyes grow larger as I ordered practically half the menu.

"You weren't joking," he said when the waiter left, though there was still a smile on his face. Either he wasn't actually mad, or he was better than most people at hiding his anger.

I stirred a straw around in my water, listening to the ice cubes clinking against each other.

"First thing to learn about me. I'm not a funny person, and I don't joke. If you do catch me joking, then you should run. That usually means I'm on my last nerve."

"I'll keep that in mind."

I couldn't bear to look at the other man's smiling face anymore.

Seriously, did he ever get upset or show any other emotion?

No one could be this pleasant all the time. It set my teeth on edge because I couldn't figure out what he was thinking.

Rather than focusing on Logan sitting across from me at the table, I watched the other people around us. It was mostly couples, and a few families with young kids. The few individual customers sat up at the bar at the front, perching on stools rather than taking up a while booth.

What did people think of us when they

saw Logan and I together?

Did they think we were a couple?

Or maybe just a pair of friends on a road trip?

We definitely didn't look related.

I noticed our waiter on the far side of the diner, whispering with other members of the staff. I initially chalked it up to typical workplace gossip, until I noticed them glaring over toward our table in between their words.

At first, I assumed the look was meant for me. Somehow, they must have figured out what I was, and they didn't approve of having someone of my "profession" in their establishment.

However, after a moment, I realized they weren't looking at me at all. Their glares were pointed at Logan.

Why?

I was suspicious of him, but that's because I was suspicious of everyone. So far, Logan hadn't done anything to draw such looks from normal people.

An image suddenly came to my mind, and for a moment I thought I'd accidentally slipped back into the Midnight Zone as I looked down at Logan and myself from an outside perspective.

However, it wasn't that. I had just been struck with clarity about what Logan and I must look like to other people.

He was well dressed, in a smart suit jacket that he'd paired with dark jeans to keep it casual. There was nothing spectacular about his look, but he was obviously well put together.

I, on the other hand, was a wreck. I'd left behind all my working clothes since I never wanted my brother to see me in such revealing outfits. This only left me with a few ratty pairs of sweatpants and two T-shirts. I was wearing the best of them now, but it was still a far cry from Logan's polished appearance.

Add in the black eye that was still tender to the touch, and we must look like an abuser and his victim.

It wasn't just the waiters, either. The whole diner kept sneaking us suspicious looks. I was tempted to stand up on the table and shout the truth from the top of my lungs to set everyone straight.

How dare they all care about me now?

Where was this concern when I was actually being abused?

What if their suspicions drove Logan away, and I lost my only chance at salvation?

Would any of them offer me the same help Logan had, or would they just shake their heads and pity me from a distance?

A touch on my hand startled me, making me jump. Logan leaned across the table, and I was certain he must be mad. This was the moment he would finally drop his "nice guy" act and show me his real face.

Yet, he just kept smiling as he cupped my hand in his own. I hadn't even realized my hands were clenched into tight fists on the table, but my fingers ached from the strain as he gently coaxed them into uncurling.

"It's all right."

I watched, distracted, as he rubbed the ache out of my fingers.

"What?"

He moved on to my other hand and soothed that one as well.

"I don't care what anyone else thinks about me. You know the truth, and I know the truth. That's enough."

"But..." He finished with the other hand and set it back down on the table, leaving behind an oddly empty feeling in my chest. "What if you get in trouble?

Those kinds of accusations could ruin your reputation."

Logan just shrugged again and started folding the paper wrapper from his straw into a complicated little coil.

"Do you plan on accusing me of anything?"

I quickly shook my head, which earned me another smile from him.

"Then it'll be fine. I've worked in law enforcement long enough to know that making a case against someone is nearly impossible without a victim's testimony."

The coiled paper sprung from his fingers, sailing a few inches through the air, before landing in a puddle of condensation that had collected under his water glass.

I watched the slowly dissolving paper with a raised eyebrow.

"Law enforcement? I thought you were a private investigator."

His face turned a shocking shade of red, and he ran a nervous hand through his hair. "Yeah. About that. I need to come clean about something. I'm not actually a private investigator."

My hand immediately went to my bag sitting on the seat beside me, ready to bolt out of that diner.

"No, wait. Let me explain." Logan waved both hands in front of himself like he was building a wall, begging me to stay without touching me. "I wasn't lying about your brother. He did hire private investigators. Damien Anderson and Sebastian Roth own *Alias Investigations*. They are private investigators, and they're the ones your brother went to. They were busy with other cases and weren't having much luck finding you, so they asked me for help."

I let go of my bag, but I remained stiff as stone on my side of the booth.

"Why you?"

"I'm, um..." He cleared his throat and wouldn't look me directly in the eye. "Back in Baton Rouge, I'm a detective with a special force called the Federal Protection Agency. It's similar to the SVU department. But I have access to... more resources for solving cases like yours."

"Baton Rouge?"

When I first escaped my captors, I'd found myself in the middle of nowhere. Even now, I still couldn't point the location out on a map. I'd walked until I found a bus terminal and bought the cheapest ticket I could find. Then I immediately fell asleep on the bus until it dumped me in Baton Rouge.

"Dinah's Place," I remembered out loud.

Logan nodded along, finally looking back up at me. "Yeah. I've had dealings with her before, so we have some rapport. I knew how to get her to talk to me, and she pointed me toward San Francisco."

I barely remembered those days. I'd been in such a daze, constantly slipping in and out of the Midnight Zone. A vague memory came to mind of asking for a job at *Dinah's Place*, then asking for help buying a bus ticket when she turned me down, but I wasn't sure if that memory was accurate or not.

"I'm surprised anyone there remembered me. That was years ago."

Logan didn't look embarrassed anymore, but a flush still stained his cheeks.

"It's not surprising. You're a hard person to forget."

Was that a compliment?

An insult?

I honestly wasn't sure which I would prefer.

Luckily, I was saved from responding by the arrival of our food. Our waiter glared at Logan the entire time, but never said a word as they dropped off plate after plate of food until the entire table was covered.

I no longer cared about judging stares or painful memories. All my attention was focused on my stomach.

Grabbing the nearest plate, which turned out to be a cheeseburger, I immediately started eating. I barely came up for air between bites as I cleaned the entire plate, fries and all, in less than two minutes.

I couldn't remember the last time I didn't feel hungry. Over the years, I'd learned to ignore the constant hunger, but now that there was a literal feast laid out before my eyes, my stomach had become a bottomless pit.

As soon as the cheeseburger was gone, I grabbed a bowl of soup and drank it down so quickly I barely tasted it.

Logan forgot all about his own food as he watched me. I waited for him to say something, to protest or chastise me for my appalling table manners, but he said nothing. He even started pushing the plates closer to me one at a time, so they'd be easier to reach.

I didn't manage to eat everything, but I polished off a significant amount of it and had the rest boxed up to take with me for later. Nearly two hours had passed when we finally left the diner. I fell asleep in the car before we even pulled out of the parking lot, warmed by the afternoon sun and the weight of my first full belly in years.

CHAPTER TEN

Clay

WE DROVE THE rest of the day and didn't stop until well after sunset. We'd just crossed from California into Nevada, and the long strip of desert ahead of us was completely barren. There wasn't even a rest stop or a gas station. It was not the kind of place to try crossing in the dead of night, so we decided to stop and resume our journey in the morning.

The little desert town we managed to find also didn't have much. There would be no fancy hotels for us that night, but at least there was a motel with some vacancies. The room even came with a fridge for me to store my leftovers from lunch, so we wouldn't have to worry about breakfast in the morning.

I was feeling surprisingly optimistic, until I stepped through the door and was greeted with the sight of a single king-size bed.

Right.

Of course.

It was as I expected. No one just gave away things for free.

I glanced over at Logan as he locked the motel door behind us.

Well, at least he was attractive. That would make things easier. I'd thought the same thing when I first met him, back in a San Francisco hotel, and here I was in the same position again.

Dropping my bag off in a nearby chair, I combed my fingers through my hair a few times to detangle it, then laid myself down on the bed.

"Sorry about the room," he said as he hung up his jacket on the peg by the door. "It's..." He trailed off when he turned around and saw me.

I refused to squirm under his attention.

I was a professional, damn it. I should

be used to this.

"Well, here we are." With one hand, I slid the bottom of my shirt up until most of my stomach was exposed. "So, what'd you want?"

He didn't move or say anything as he continued to stare at me.

I wanted to scream at him.

What was he waiting for?

Just get it over with already.

Did he want me to beg, or play coy?

Some clients only enjoyed it if they could delude themselves into thinking I wanted it as well. Maybe Logan was one of those.

I sat up on my knees and bit my lip, looking him up and down with my best look of desperation.

Yet, just as I opened my mouth to start begging, he held up a hand to silence me.

"I'm sorry. I think there's been a misunderstanding. This was the only kind of room they had available. But..."

He looked around at the room, taking in the walls, the cracked television, and even the bathroom door. Everywhere but in my direction.

"I'll, um... I'll go sleep in the car."

He was already reached for the door

handle before I spoke up.

"Wait." I sighed and reached out to grab his arm, tugging him toward the bed. "Don't sleep in the car. You've been driving all day. That isn't fair."

He didn't leave, but he also didn't approach the bed.

"I'd rather sleep in the car than stay here and make you uncomfortable."

"I'm not..."

Growling in frustration, I stood abruptly from the bed and started rooting through my bag of meager possessions.

"I'm not uncomfortable. I'm just..."

When I finally located a mostly clean change of clothes, I headed for the bathroom, but stopped at the door to look back at him over my shoulder.

"Look. Every instinct I have says that you must want something from me. I can't help it. I expect you to try and take advantage of me. So, sleep in the bed. If you do try something with me, then it's exactly what I expected. If you don't, then I'll be pleasantly surprised. It's entirely up to you."

Before he could respond, I slipped inside the bathroom and quickly closed the door behind me. The shower barely had any water pressure, and it didn't get very hot, but I was more interested in the distraction of a shower than actually getting clean.

Anger prickled under my skin as I washed my hair, but I couldn't tell who I was angry at.

Logan?

Myself?

The situation in general?

My thoughts weren't clear enough to give me a straight answer. The emotions running through me seemed to have no rhyme or reason.

I grumbled under my breath as I finished washing my hair and scrubbed every inch of my skin with the cheap soap provided by the motel.

As the hot water ran out and my shower turned cold, so did my anger. When I finally stepped out of the shower, I was just tired.

Tired and numb, like all my emotions had disappeared down the shower drain with the rest of the water.

I just wanted to sleep. Alone or not didn't even matter anymore. I rushed to dry myself off and put on the clean set of clothes before heading back to the bedroom.

While I'd been showering, Logan had turned off the lights and climbed into bed, laying as close to the edge of the mattress as he could with his back facing me. I could tell he wasn't asleep yet, but he didn't say a word as I slipped under the sheet beside him.

For a while, I lay there in the dark, waiting for him to turn over and reach for me. I wouldn't even care if he did. I had no emotions left, other than a numb sense of curiosity.

Yet, the minutes ticked by, and he didn't move or even acknowledge me next to him. Eventually, I heard his breathing pattern change, and I knew he'd fallen asleep.

Turning over to face the opposite wall, I hugged the remaining pillow to my chest and closed my eyes. Part of me was relieved that he hadn't tried to touch me, but part of me was confused and even a little disappointed.

I felt like an actor that had gone through the effort of memorizing all their lines, only to step out onto the stage and find my costar acting out an entirely different play.

I'd gladly say the right lines if someone would just give me the correct script.

Despite my earlier nap, I was still exhausted, and it didn't take long for me to drift off to sleep.

My last thought was a vague hope that maybe everything would make more sense in the morning.

CHAPTER ELEVEN

Logan

WE CROSSED THE next two states without incident and left the desert and mountains behind for the Great Plains. The area certainly lived up to its name.

It was great, and it was plain.

The change of scenery was refreshing at first, but endless flat green grasslands soon grew very boring.

On the afternoon of the third day of our trip, we were somewhere in Nevada, and Clay was sitting beside me scrolling through my phone for music worth listening to. I hadn't prepared for a long road trip, so I didn't have much ready to go, but Clay seemed to find some amusement building a playlist on my Spotify account.

"Seriously, do you pick things by just spinning a wheel. You have the most random music history." Clay scowled at something on my phone, then started laughing. "You listened to several country songs and then immediately switched over to Rhianna. Why? What do those possibly have in common?"

Clay's laughter was genuine, and it chased away any annoyance I felt about making such a long trip. I didn't even care that he was finding joy in making fun of me. It was the first time I'd seen him actually enjoying something, and I wasn't going to ruin it.

It wasn't even the first time someone had made fun of my music choices, either. Those kinds of jokes were common amongst my friends.

I couldn't explain it, either. When I was listening to music my mind was free to wander, and it would latch onto the most random things. A single lyric in one song would remind me of something completely different, and I wouldn't be able to get it out of my head until I found it.

Online algorithms hated me. They could never predict what I wanted, which led to some awkward content suggestions.

Clay laughed again, this time having found a time in my history when I spent several days skipping between show tunes, barely letting one finish before moving onto the next.

It was a good thing I was driving. The task gave me something to distract myself, so I wouldn't spend the trip just staring at him. Clay was so much more beautiful when he was happy. Even his black eye, which had faded to an ugly shade of yellow and green, seemed to soften around the edges.

I kept my eyes fixed resolutely on the road. There was no way I could avoid looking at him entirely, so I watched the clock, and allowed myself one brief glance over at him once every ten minutes.

I'd been hoping to get most of the way through Nevada by the end of the day, but the weather had other plans. Seemingly in the blink of an eye, the sunny sky turned dark and cloudy. The bright afternoon light was chased away, and we were plunged into a gloomy dark that made it feel more like twilight.

As the rain started, we pressed on, hoping the storm would pass, but soon it was coming down so hard I could barely see the road in front of me.

"We're going to have to pull over early today," I declared as I squinted to try and make out the road lines.

I was certain I was still on the road based on the feeling of the ground under my tires, but I couldn't be certain what lane I was in.

Clay didn't argue, and even seemed relieved as he directed our GPS to the nearest motel.

We were crawling down the road at a snail's pace through the rain. Despite the nearest motel being only two miles away, nearly an hour passed before we pulled into the parking lot.

I couldn't even read the motel's neon sign through the downpour, and hoped they had vacancies, otherwise we'd be sleeping in the car. Until the storm passed, we weren't going anywhere.

The car was a rental, and I hadn't planned ahead enough to bring an umbrella, so Clay and I darted across the parking lot toward the motel's front awning as quickly as we could.

"Stupid, fucking rain," Clay complained once we were safely under cover. "Storms shouldn't be able to just roll in without warning like that."

He finger-combed the water from his hair, pushing it back out of his face. The rain had turned his hair to a dark honey color, which complimented his blue eyes well.

A drop of rainwater traveled down his neck toward his collarbone. I tracked its path for a moment, before realizing what I was doing and quickly turning away.

"Are you coming in?" I asked as I held the front door open for him.

He shook his head and started shaking out his shirt to keep it from clinging uncomfortably to his skin. "No. I'd rather stay out here. Wet clothes and air-conditioning don't mix."

By now, I was certain that he wasn't going to suddenly disappear or run away, so I felt comfortable enough to leave him alone for a few minutes.

Still, I vowed to hurry back as I headed for the motel's front desk.

The person sitting behind the counter barely looked up from their phone when I approached and just waved toward a sign with their rates posted.

It all looked standard, and I was about to request a room for the night—with two beds this time—when I noticed something written at the bottom of the sign.

It was listed so matter-of-factly that I hadn't even noticed at first, but apparently the motel also offered rooms that could be rented by the hour.

There was only one reason to rent a room in such a way. People either brought their partner here for a clandestine affair, or they brought someone that they'd paid for.

How many hours had Clay spent in places just like this?

The question slipped into my mind like a highly trained assassin. With no warning, my thoughts took on a dark edge, and the once normal looking motel took on a sinister outlook. The staff behind the desk, who barely looked at me, now seemed to be leering at me out of the corner of their eye, and I swore I could feel the shadows in the corner of the room creeping closer.

I quickly paid for a single night, not even looking at the price as I handed over my credit card, and returned to Clay outside as soon as possible.

He wasn't alone. While I'd been gone, a man had approached him, and was now leaning way too close into Clay's personal space as he spoke.

"Ah, come on. I've already bought the room for us. You can't change your mind now."

Clay backed away from him and looked to be only moments away from punching the man. "You've got the wrong person. I'm not here for you."

Instead of taking the hint, the man only pushed closer.

"Don't be like that, Angel. What? You find a better client or something? I'll match whatever they're offering."

I expected Clay to shove him away, maybe even hit him, but instead Clay stood completely unmoving as the man's hand started trailing up his thigh.

Snapping out of my own shock, I grabbed the back of the man's jacket and pulled him away. "Hey! He told you to leave. Get lost."

I tossed the man out into the rain so he landed in a puddle and stood in front of Clay's frozen figure so the stranger wouldn't be able to see him.

Clambering off the ground, the man threw water everywhere as he puffed up like an angry bull.

"Bastard. I was here first, and I already paid upfront. You can't just steal from me."

As a detective, a concealed-carry permit came with my job. I took advantage of that benefit now and pulled out the gun I kept hidden in a secret pocket inside my jacket.

"He already told you that you have the wrong person. So, start listening and fuck off."

The moment the barrel of the gun pointed toward him; the man's anger instantly deflated. Holding up his hands, he slowly backed away.

"Hey, man. It's cool. You can have him. I'll just... go somewhere else."

"I'm not—" I started to say, but the man had already left. He probably wouldn't have believed me if I tried to argue with him anyway, so I let him go and turned back today.

"All right. He's gone."

Clay didn't answer. He just stood there, staring blankly into space as if his muscles had suddenly turned to stone.

"Hey, Clay." I waved a hand in front of his face. "You okay?"

Still no response.

At first, I thought Clay might be reacting to the sight of the gun and quickly hid it away again, but even once the gun was out of sight, Clay's reaction didn't change.

Then it hit me.

Angel.

The man had called Clay "Angel".

Jordie had warned me about using that word. I knew Clay hated the name, and for good reason, but I hadn't realized his reaction would be this bad.

He was completely catatonic.

It wasn't the first time I'd seen a victim triggered by something that reminded them of their trauma. In fact, those kinds of PTSD reactions were unfortunately common. However, that felt like more than just trauma resurfacing. The reaction had been too sudden, like a switch had been flipped.

It felt... like a conditioned response.

"Hey, Clay. It's okay." I put my hand on his shoulder, hoping to snap him out of whatever flashback he'd fallen into, but the moment my hand made contact he lashed out and shoved me away.

"Don't touch me."

Holding up both my hands, I backed away, but that only distressed him even more.

"No, wait." He grabbed my sleeve and pulled me back. "Don't leave. Sorry... I'm not..."

"It's okay," I said again, keeping my voice as low and smooth as I could. "I'm not going anywhere. Let's just get out of the rain and somewhere warm. Okay?"

He nodded but didn't say anything as he continued to cling to my sleeve. I didn't dare touch him again, not knowing what kind of response I'd get, so I used his grip on my sleeve to bring him with me as I fetched our stuff from the car and headed for our room.

There were two beds this time, luckily. I wasn't sure how he would react to sleeping in the same bed right now, and I couldn't risk upsetting him further.

Leading him over to the other bed, I detached his hands from my sleeve and handed him his own bag.

"Here. You need to get out of those wet clothes and dry off. I'm going to go change in the bathroom."

Once his fingers wrapped around the handle of his bag, I grabbed my own stuff and locked myself in the bathroom. I wanted to take a shower to chase away the chill after getting soaked, but I also couldn't leave Clay alone for too long in his current state.

Drying myself off with a towel, I slipped on a new set of clothes and returned to the bedroom, only to immediately turn around again.

"Clay, what... are you doing?"

I should have been more specific with my instructions. He'd stripped himself out of his wet clothes, but now stood naked in the center of the room, looking lost and vacant.

With a sigh, I kept my eyes averted as I sidled up closer to him without looking directly at him.

"Clay. Get dressed." Bending down, I managed to grab his bag and hand it to him, but after that I didn't hear any movement.

When nearly a minute had passed with seemingly nothing happening, I snuck another look at him, focusing only on his face.

He held his bag of supplies, looking at

it with clear confusion, like he knew he needed to do something, but couldn't figure out how to navigate the maze of his own body to make it happen.

Then he gave up and dropped the bag to latch onto my sleeve again.

I sighed. This was going to be a long night.

It was a small room, so the beds weren't too far away. I was able to pull the blanket off of one without leaving Clay's side and wrapped it around the younger man like a warm dry cocoon.

"There," I said as I used the towel I'd brought from the bathroom to dry his hair. "That should feel better."

He responded by leaning his head against my chest. There were only a few inches of difference between our height, so he had to duck a little for his head to fit under my chin.

I expected him to cry. He certainly had plenty of reasons to cry. However, instead, he wrapped his arms around me tightly and screamed against my chest.

Even with his voice muffled into my shirt I could still hear his shouting and feel the vibration in his voice. His screams mixed with sobs, twisting into a tortured sound that would haunt my nightmares for years to come.

I didn't react, and just continued to hold him, even as his pain overflowed into his fists. He beat against my chest and shoulders, still screaming the whole time.

I was going to have bruises there in the morning, but I bit my lip and forced myself to keep quiet. I could handle a few bruises. It was a worthwhile price to pay if it helped Clay express even a fraction of the pain and anger that must be poisoning him from the inside.

His outburst lasted for several minutes before he finally fell silent and stood slumped in my arms. At a higher-end hotel someone would have probably called security on us by now, but that was one of the only good things about our current location.

No one was going to complain about the sound of screams.

"Sorry," Clay said with his face still lying against my chest. "I don't know why I did that. I shouldn't... I just... Sorry."

His whole body was trembling in my arms. He was exhausted, but he was still trying to keep himself standing.

I led him over to one of the beds,

helping him lie down while keeping the blanket cocoon safely tucked around him.

"It's fine. Don't apologize for having emotions. You should feel free to be as sad or as angry as you want."

The sight of his blue eyes peeking out of the blanket was unbearably cute.

Or it would have been if his eyes weren't red-rimmed from crying.

His face wasn't covered by the blanket, but his voice still sounded very quiet when he spoke up. "It doesn't make any sense. I shouldn't be angry now."

I sat next to him on the bed, keeping to the edge so some space remained between us. "You're allowed to be angry."

Clay snorted and looked away. "Yeah, maybe. But I shouldn't be. There's no reason for that guy to upset me so much. It's certainly not the first time someone's gotten handsy with me, and it's not even the first time I've been called... that name. I don't know why it affected me so strongly this time when I've never broken down like that in the past."

He re-settled himself, so his arms were outside the blanket. A few scars curled over the tops of his shoulders, and although I couldn't see them properly, I was certain they extended further down his back.

The thin lines looked like whip marks.

I turned my eyes away before I was caught staring and refocused on the conversation.

"You said you never got so upset before. Maybe that's why. All those negative emotions have been building up with nowhere to go."

He huffed, and for a moment it seemed like he wanted to turn away from me, but he didn't. "Why now? I should be happy I'm finally getting away from that life. What's the point in getting upset about everything now that I'm leaving it behind?"

That was the first time Clay had talked about his relocation as a permanent change. Until now, he always spoke like he was visiting his brother. Just a temporary guest that would go right back to the status quo of their life when the visit was over.

To hear him talk about getting away and leaving everything behind caused something tangled in my chest to unknot.

"Well..." I thought about a good answer for a moment, and I could only come up with one thing. "Hopefully, getting upset know means you feel safe enough to express those emotions."

Clay was silent, biting his lip as he got lost in thought.

"You are safe."

His words were distracted, like he was only half paying attention to them. Some other thought was bouncing around in his head. I could almost see the thoughts passing behind his eyes, but I didn't ask. Instead, I sat in silence, listening to the room's old analog clock ticking away each passing second.

The minute hand must have gone around several times before Clay finally spoke again.

"Bell ringers."

I had no idea what that meant, but didn't ask, certain that he would explain.

He did, but it took him an obvious amount of effort to get the words out.

"That's what they called themselves. The Bell ringers."

"You mean the people who kidnapped you?"

"Yeah."

He laughed, a sad, pathetic little sound that made me want to hug him again, but I refrained.

"Every time a bell rings, an angel gets his wings." His laughter trailed off and something dark settled behind his eyes. "That's what they said, but that wasn't where the name really came from. It's about how they found us."

"How they found you? When you were kidnapped?"

Clay didn't look at me. He barely even seemed to remember I was there as he revealed the truth he'd been carrying around for almost a decade.

"They started back when door-to-door salesmen were a thing, but now they use any excuse to get into someone's house. Handymen. Surveys. They'll even pose as Mormons or Jehovah's Witnesses for an excuse to knock on people's doors. I think their favorite is pretending to be surveying gas meters. That's how they scoped me out. No one questions a person in a uniform with a clipboard, so they can come and go as they please and get all the info on their target."

I tried not to react, but there must have been a strange expression on my face. When I'd initially investigated the pedophile ring that kidnapped Clay, I'd never been able to figure out how they found their victims. There seemed to be no crossover or similarities between the victims, other than their physical appearance, and without this crucial piece of info, the investigation had stalled.

I'd also never known they had been operating for so long. Based on Clay's description, they'd probably been targeting kids for decades. Long enough for them to give themselves a title, as if they were a legitimate organization.

In their twisted minds, they probably were.

Breathing deeply and biting the inside of my cheek, I controlled my reaction so I didn't startle Clay. He likely didn't realize the importance of what he'd revealed. He didn't need that added stress on top of everything. Investigating criminals was my responsibility and I would handle it.

Clay's eyes were drooping. Although he was trying to stay awake, after his emotional outburst, he no longer had the energy to continue that fight and was quickly succumbing to sleep.

After wishing him a good night, I stood to leave, already reaching into my pocket to grab my phone so I could pass on the information I'd just learned.

Before I could make it even a foot from the bed, something tugged on my sleeve. I looked down to find Clay nervously glancing at me from the corner of his eye, like he couldn't bear to stare straight at me.

"Could you... could you stay?"

"Stay?" I eyed the empty side of his bed. "Is that a good idea?"

"I just—"

His expression suddenly smoothed out, like someone had ironed all the emotion out of his skin leaving nothing but blank thoughtlessness behind. "Never mind. It's stupid. You'll be more comfortable in your own bed."

At the sight of that blank look on his face, all my doubts vanished. Without another word, I turned off the room lights and slipped under the covers beside him. The bed was big enough that we didn't have to touch so long as we each kept to our side, so I moved the pillow as close to the edge as I could without falling off.

At first, Clay didn't even acknowledge me, and I was content to be ignored the rest of the night. However, after a few minutes, tentative fingers gripped onto my shirt.

"Thanks."

That was all he said, though it was already more than I expected. There were plenty of phone calls I would need to make in the morning. I should at least call Roland, as he had worked the "Bell ringer" case with me and would be able to get started investigating the new information immediately, and it would probably be a good idea to tell Sebastian as well, since he was pursuing a similar case.

For tonight, however, I was happy to play the role of guard dog.

CHAPTER TWELVE

Clay

LOGAN'S RANDOM SELECTION of music had landed us on a selection of eighties music. The morning of the sixth day of our trip was spent rocking out to songs from *Madonna, Guns N' Roses,* and *Duran Duran.* Logan never asked why I curated the music before listening to it, but I could tell he knew the reason.

"Angel" was an unfortunately common word that popped up in many lyrics. Like walking through a field laced with hidden landmines. If I didn't already know the song, I could be enjoying myself one minute, then trip right into an explosion of unwanted memories.

I used to love Christmas as a kid, but now the season put me into a constant state of anxiety due to all the angel imagery.

Michael Jackson's song *Beat It* had just ended, with Logan and I singing along out of turn, when we passed a sign that said, "Welcome to Maryland." Since my breakdown a few days ago, I'd stopped paying attention to the miles passing by and just enjoyed my time with Logan. It had been so long since I actually felt safe with someone that nothing else seemed to matter. I'd nearly forgotten the reason we were driving to Maryland in the first place.

There was only about two hundred miles between us and our destination.

Two hundred miles until I saw my brother again.

Panic surged hot in my gut, and I could taste the pancakes I'd had for breakfast coming back up again.

"Pull over."

I had no idea what my face looked like, but it must have been dramatic. Logan didn't even wait to find a rest stop, and just pulled immediately over to the side of the freeway.

I stumbled out of the door before the car had even been put in park and ran to the side of the road to throw up over the concrete barrier.

My throat burned with bile, and my eyes were watering so badly that the world looked blurry around me. Through it all, Logan's hand trailed over my back, soothing my fevered skin even through my clothes.

"Sorry," I croaked as I stood back up. By now, I wasn't even surprised when Logan's only response was to hand me a tissue to wipe my mouth and a bottle of water.

We stood there for about fifteen minutes by the side of the road, waiting for me to compose myself. Part of me wanted to immediately get back in the car and finish the trip while another part of me wanted to run in the other direction away from this whole crazy idea before I could get hurt again.

Because this was certainly going to hurt.

There was no way my brother would accept me back into his life. He might claim to accept me and understand what

I'd been through, but that was easy to say from a distance. The reality would be very different when I was standing in front of him and I was no longer the same unbroken kid he remembered.

"What if he doesn't want me? I don't have anywhere else to go. At least back in San Francisco I had a roof over my head. Here, I'll be broke and homeless."

While we'd been waiting, Logan had grabbed a water bottle for himself as well. He took a deep sip, giving my question proper consideration before answering.

"I don't think you need to worry about that. From what I've seen of Jason Dahler, he seems like a reasonable man." Just as I was about to argue, Logan cut me off. "However, if it turns out I'm wrong and you aren't able to stay here..." He shrugged. "Then, I'll just have to take you somewhere else. It's a big world. There are plenty of places you could go. Heck. I've even got a guest room, if you'd like. You've got plenty of options."

My whole body was numb as I listened to him, and the water bottle slipped from my fingers. It made an unexpectedly loud sound when it hit the asphalt, but it managed to land in just the right way that it remained upright. Some of the water splashed out, but it remained, for the most part, unsullied by the dirt on the ground.

I stared at the bottle, fighting the urge to kick it over. "You'd do that? You'd really... take me with you?"

Logan bent down to pick the water bottle off the ground and screw the cap back on before storing it with his own half-finished bottle in the back of the car.

"Of course. One way or another, I'm going to see you safe and settled somewhere. However, like I said, I don't think it'll be a problem."

He stretched his arms over his head, groaning when his spine popped after so many days of driving. My gaze automatically tracked the rise of his shirt, which exposed an inch of skin just above his pants. The skin under his clothes was a little paler than on his arms and face, meaning some of his tanned complexion came from spending plenty of time in the sun.

I wondered what he did in his off time, when he wasn't rescuing lost souls and reuniting families.

Was Logan the kind of person who

enjoyed extreme outdoor activities, or was he the kind of person who kicked back on the beach and relaxed during his down time?

I'd probably never know, and that thought made me sad. Logan had a life to get back to; a life filled with people and activities I wasn't a part of.

It was time to get on with my own life.

We climbed back into the car, and finished the last two hundred miles listening to various types of classical music that filled the silence without the risk of any inflammatory lyrics.

The clock on the car's radio showed it was just past noon when we pulled into my brother's neighborhood. It wasn't the same exact same area where I'd grown up, but it was close enough that I could almost imagine I was traveling back in time. It seemed like nothing had changed in the years I'd been gone.

Jason's house looked just like the images I'd seen on social media. Even the picket fence surrounding the property was so white it looked like it had been photoshopped.

Was it better or worse that Jason's life was just as picturesque as it seemed from a distance?

Despite recognizing the house, I didn't immediately recognize my brother standing in the driveway. Jason was smiling in all his social media pictures, but now he looked stressed and worried, pacing back and forth from one end of the driveway to the other.

He looked like a completely different person without a smile on his face, but oddly enough, the fact gave me comfort.

In that condition, he looked more like me, and I could see the resemblance between us.

The car came to a stop in the driveway, but before I could get out, Logan told me to wait for a second. He got out first and went to speak with my brother. If I rolled down the window, I probably could have heard what they were saying, but I didn't want to know.

After a minute, Jason backed up a few steps, keeping some distance from the car as Logan opened the door for me.

"All right. It's now or never."

My hands shook as I held my bag to my chest, hyper-aware of how little the entirety of my possessions weighed. Stepping out of Logan's car took more effort than I cared to admit. I nearly slipped into the Midnight Zone when I heard the door close behind me. My vision started fading around the edges, and for a moment, I could see myself from above as I approached my brother, but I shoved the welcoming headspace away and focused on what was happening. I'd both hoped for and dreaded this moment for years, and I was determined to experience it with a clear head, no matter the outcome.

"Clay?" Jason said as I approached.

My name sounded like both a greeting and a question at the same time. It was no wonder. In his eyes, I must look like a creature from a horror film. Like a shape-shifting alien, or a Skinwalker trying to take his brother's place.

"Jason." His name felt awkward on my lips, but I didn't know what else to say. "Um... I'm back. I guess. Or... back doesn't really sound like the right word. I'm here? No. That's worse."

My inane rambling cut off when he grabbed my shoulders. His touch was light, I could barely feel the weight of his hands, but the sudden physical contact still made me flinch. Luckily, he didn't notice, as he was too busy looking me up and down like he was trying to see all of me at once.

After a moment of consideration, his gaze landed on my neck. The birthmark there was still the same shape as when I was a kid.

Most days, when I looked in the mirror, I didn't even recognize myself. Except for my birthmark. That always looked familiar.

Jason seemed to take comfort in the mark as well, for once he noticed it, his whole face lit up with joy.

"You're back."

Before I could respond, he pulled me into a hug.

I froze.

For a moment, my fight or flight instincts kicked in and I nearly shoved him away. That would have ruined everything, so thankfully, I was able to control it and stand still for the remainder of the hug.

When Jason pulled away, there were tears in his eyes and I could feel some dampness on my shirt. Yet, he was also smiling and he wiped the tears away with a bubbling little laugh.

"Sorry. I'm making a mess of you.

Here. Come inside. We can sit down and talk where it's more comfortable."

He held out a hand toward the front door of the house in an inviting gesture, but I looked back toward Logan.

He wasn't going to leave yet, was he?

Technically, his job was done. He'd brought me to my brother safe and sound. He was free to return to his life, back on the other side of the country.

Logan must have read the distress on my face, for he stepped up to accept my brother's invitation for me.

"Yeah. We should go inside. No reason to have this kind of conversation out on the street."

Inside, Jason's house was just as perfectly laid out as the outside, right down to the tasteful artwork on the walls and the glass vase sitting on its own display table and holding a purple orchid that was so flawless I thought it was fake at first.

I scowled at the flower. From what I'd heard about orchids, they were very difficult to maintain, and this one stood at least two feet tall with many colorful blooms.

How much time and effort went into

caring for this single plant?

It was living better than a lot of people I knew, including myself. The imbalance didn't seem fair.

"Hello."

I jumped at the sound of the unexpected voice, and barely avoided knocking over the vase.

Off to the side, another person stood in the living room, obviously waiting for us. The man's face was familiar, but it took me a moment to recognize him.

Jason approached the other man with a wide smile and open arms. "Clay. Let me introduce you to my partner, Patrick."

Patrick was a sturdy looking individual, with soft eyes and an endearingly crooked smile. He accepted a brief one-armed hug from Jason, the kind of familiar show of intimacy only exchanged by couples. Then, he approached me with a smile on his face and his hand outstretched. "Clay. It's great to finally meet you. Jason has told me so much about you. I'm glad you're finally here."

"Right." I accepted his handshake, but my own hand was limp with shock and probably felt like a dead fish in comparison to his firm, confident grip. "Sorry. I forgot."

"Forgot?" Jason asked as he stepped up to Patrick's side.

"That you're married. I forgot you're married. Congratulations. Sorry, I'm three years too late to congratulate you."

An expression fell over Jason's face that I couldn't read. His eyebrows were pinched together in a way that implied unhappy thoughts, but he didn't exactly look upset.

Had I said something wrong?

Did my comment about congratulating him remind him of how much time had passed?

Surely, they didn't think I'd have a problem with their relationship. Even if I wasn't also gay myself, I'd have no cause to complain about a relationship that made my brother happy.

"You... know when we got married?" Jason asked.

"Oh, um, yeah." I shrugged. "I've looked you up online before, so I've kept track of the important things."

"Important things? But you didn't..." Whatever Jason was going to say, he stopped himself and shook his head before his expression abruptly shifted. "Come on. Sit down. Tell us about your drive here."

When Jason sat down, a small dog jumped onto his lap, happily wagging its tail. It was a white, moppet-like thing. Probably a purebred, but I didn't know enough about dogs to recognize which one. It didn't even seem to notice me, so focused on getting attention from its owner.

Jason's hand automatically stroked over the dog's back as he spoke. "We've already got the guest room made up. You can move your stuff in there immediately. Is the rest of it in the car?"

I glanced down at the single bag sitting by my feet. "No. This is it."

"Ah." Jason's expression shuttered for a moment, his smile nearly slipping off before latching on more firmly again. "That certainly makes moving easier. Did you have a hard time getting here?"

Did I?

My first instinct was to say no. Logan had done all the work driving, and even paid for everything. All I had to do was sit in the passenger seat and pick out music to listen to.

However, I also couldn't say it had been easy. I'd had more breakdowns in the last few days than in the last several years.

When the silence lasted too long and I still hadn't said anything, Logan took over and answered Jason's question for me. He gave a general explanation of our trip, focusing on mundane things like the different scenery we'd passed, and having to pull over when we got caught in the storm. Not once did he mention any of my tantrums, or the numerous times I'd broken down crying, or throwing up on the side of the road. Based on Logan's description, it almost sounded like we were on a vacation exploring the countryside.

This was how conversations were supposed to be. Small talk was meant to fill the silence between people and put everyone at ease. It seemed to take Logan no effort at all, as if he already knew exactly what to say and what not to say.

When had I lost the ability to carry on a conversation?

How was I supposed to live here if I couldn't even talk to my own brother without being frozen with indecision?

The conversation around me died and the silence alerted me to the fact that something was wrong. Snapping out of my thoughts, I noticed everyone looking at me with concern.

Even the damned dog had stopped wagging its tail to stare at me with its big dark eyes.

Logan's hand gripped my shoulder. "Clay? What's wrong?"

That was when I felt the moisture dripping down my cheeks. Somewhere during the conversation I'd begun to cry silently without even noticing.

Something in my chest clicked, like a lock falling open, and I started openly sobbing and blabbering all at once. Every thought I'd had since arriving all tumbled out of my mouth at once. The confusing mix of hope and fear that had been plaguing me since the start of the journey here was difficult to explain, and probably didn't make much sense. Especially since I was trying to talk with my face buried in my hands to hide my tears.

Yet, no one tried to stop me or told me to be quiet.

Several minutes passed before I calmed down enough to look up and wipe the tears out of my eyes. I found Logan sitting beside me, as I'd come to expect, but I was more surprised to find my brother also kneeling on the floor in front of me. His hand rested on the couch cushion next to my leg, like he'd tried to reach out but hadn't wanted to touch me.

"Sorry," I muttered as I used the sleeve of my shirt to scrub the moisture off my face. "I didn't mean to ruin the mood like that. Just ignore me. I'm a mess."

The bruise around my eye had faded but had not completely disappeared. It had stopped throbbing after about two days, and I could almost forget about it so long as I didn't look in a mirror. However, my furious scrubbing at my face reminded me that the old wound was still there. I flinched when I pressed too hard near my eye, but kept going, desperate to erase the evidence of my most recent outburst.

A hand on my wrist stopped my movements. Jason was careful as he pulled my hands away from my face, not gripping me too hard so I could pull away if I wanted to.

"Please don't apologize. You didn't ruin anything. I expected today to be emotional. In fact, I'd be more worried if you didn't cry."

"But—" I couldn't decide whether to push his hands away or hold onto him, so I ended up just making a strange pointless gesture like I was trying to grasp something that didn't exist. "You seemed so excited about me coming here. I don't want to make you upset. This should be a happy moment, right?"

"This moment shouldn't even exist."

I pulled back at the unexpected rejection, but almost as soon as he spoke Jason seemed to realize how his words sounded and rushed to correct himself.

"No, wait. I don't mean you shouldn't be here. I mean, we shouldn't need to be reunited at all. You shouldn't have been missing in the first place. But we can't change the past, and you're here now. That's all that matters. Happy. Sad. Angry. I don't care as long as you're here."

Jason had always been taller than me, even when we were kids. I couldn't remember a moment when I wasn't looking up to him. Yet, with him kneeling on the floor, I was the taller of the two of us for once. That made it much easier when I leaned forward and pulled him into a hug.

As soon as I crossed that physical boundary, Jason's arms wrapped around me so tightly my ribs ached. It was technically our second hug, but with both of us participating, it put our first hug to shame.

We didn't cry. Enough tears had already been shed today. I couldn't even describe the emotions swirling through me as I held my brother for the first time in years. They weren't all happy emotions, but they weren't all negative ones, either.

Logan's hand on my shoulder caught my attention, and I looked over at him without breaking the hug.

He silently mouthed a question toward me, asking me if I was okay.

I thought for a moment, then gave a small nod.

I wasn't great, but I was okay. My brother accepted me, and seemed to have even made a place for me in his home.

That was enough for now.

CHAPTER THIRTEEN

Clay

THE SUN HAD already set an hour ago as I walked the calm suburban streets that were becoming increasingly familiar. In the two weeks since I'd arrived at my brother's, an evening walk had become my regular routine. I told myself it was in order to get to know the neighborhood around Jason's house, but that was a lie.

It was my only excuse to get out of the house.

I'd been living with my brother and his husband for two weeks. Logan had left the same day he dropped me off, after making sure I would be okay, and I'd been settling in ever since. It felt like a year had passed since then, but also the blink of an eye at the same time. Each day seemed to drag on, yet when I looked back, I couldn't believe so many had already passed.

I had been found, but I also felt more lost than ever. When I lived in San Francisco, every day had the exact same purpose. Make enough money to keep living until tomorrow. Now, without that constant motivator hanging over my head, I had no idea what to do.

The lap I took around the neighborhood lasted for about half an hour, depending on which path I chose that night. Turning onto Jason's street, I could see his house in the distance, lit up from the inside with warm, happy light like a beacon summoning me back.

Jason didn't rush me to do anything. He didn't even ask me to pay rent. After getting me set up in the guest room, it had quickly been dubbed "my" room as if I owned it, and that had been that.

He didn't push, but he also didn't leave me alone.

He ran a successful construction company, so he was a busy man, but whenever he was home, I could hear him pacing back and forth outside my door every few minutes, like he kept forgetting I was there and needed to double check.

I appreciated it, especially on late nights when I woke up from a nightmare and the sound of his footsteps reminded me where I was.

The front porch was sturdy under my feet as I climbed up to the door of Jason's house. There wasn't a single creaky board or loose stone to trip me up.

Had Jason built it himself?

Probably.

The foundation was sturdy, and if it was an example of his company's typical work, it was no wonder he was doing so well.

It still felt strange to open the front door with my own key. It had been given to me on my second day there, with a promise that I could come and go as I pleased. So far, Jason had lived up to that promise, but it didn't really matter.

Where would I even go?

Kent Island may have been my hometown at one point, but it was a stranger to me now. Just like with Jason, we hadn't grown together, and had to rebuild our familiarity from scratch.

Once inside the house, I crept quietly toward my room, but was stopped by the sound of voices in the kitchen.

Jason and Patrick were there, speaking together in hushed tones as they cleaned up the dishes from dinner. I would have left them alone to their domesticity, but the sound of my own name caught my attention.

"We need to do something with him," Patrick said, his voice barely audible over the clinking of plates and the rush of running water.

"Do what? He just got here. He needs time to get used to things."

"He needs time, sure, but he'll never get used to things if he just sits up in his room all day. Some days, I don't think he even wakes up. That's not healthy."

I stepped back behind the shadow of the doorway to ensure they wouldn't see me, even if they looked in my direction. That meant I couldn't see what they were doing, but the clinking of plates suddenly stopped.

"Healthy?" Jason's voice sounded strangled when he spoke, as if someone had a hand around his throat. "None of this is healthy. There's nothing healthy about a bunch of adults kidnapping a child so they can… so they can…"

His voice grew weaker and weaker until it failed all together. Then the sound of the running water turned off as well and the kitchen was mostly silent.

"I know." Patrick's voice was incredibly soft, and nearly brought tears to my eyes just from the sound. "It's a lot, and this has all happened so suddenly. You've been looking for him for years, and suddenly he's here. It's going to be an adjustment, but that doesn't mean we can just let him sit up there all alone every day. Even if he doesn't want to, he needs to start doing something."

I clenched my hands at my sides as I was overcome with the instinct to barge into that kitchen and give Patrick a piece of my mind.

Who the hell was he to tell me what I could or couldn't do?

Even clients that paid for my time never dared to try and dictate what I could do when I was alone.

As soon as it came over me, the anger fled, and a sad emptiness was left in its place. Even such a small flare of emotion drained me, and I immediately wanted to go back to sleep.

Turning away from the kitchen, I headed for my room, but I stopped when my gaze landed on the bookcase near the bottom of the stairs.

Maybe I should grab a few books to take with me. Reading would at least give me something to do, as Jason and Patrick apparently wanted.

Admittedly, I had been sleeping a lot. Either that or sitting up in my room staring out the window at the passing cars and pedestrians walking their dogs. Reading could be a good change of pace.

Most of the books on the shelf were either hefty detective novels, or non-fiction. Neither of which really appealed to me.

Back in San Francisco, I had a library card, but because of my living conditions, I could never risk bringing any books home. I'd only been able to read at the library, whenever my schedule allowed enough free time. This wasn't very often, but the few times I'd found a free afternoon to sit and read, I'd been disheartened by the experience.

Reading a full novel was a lot harder

than I expected. It was incredibly difficult for me to concentrate on a book for more than ten or fifteen minutes at a time before I started to feel drained. Because of that, I hadn't visited the library as often as I probably should have, and when I did, I usually stuck to short stories, or books with plenty of pictures to enhance the story.

I didn't want to admit it, but I'd lost a lot of my reading ability over the years. I'd never even graduated middle school, and my captors hadn't been concerned with keeping up my education. While I hadn't been illiterate before I was kidnapped, I'd lost much of the skill due to a lack of practice.

It was just one more thing that had been taken from me, and I hadn't even realized I'd lost it until it was gone.

What else had I lost without knowing it?

As I scanned the bookshelf, I eventually managed to find a title that looked mildly interesting. It seemed to be something about pirates, though I couldn't tell if it was meant to be a fictional story or a historical account.

Still, pirates had to be interesting, so I

grabbed the book off the shelf.

Unfortunately, I hadn't realized that the angle it was sitting at had been propping up several other books. When I removed it, most of the books on the shelf tumbled off and crashed to the floor.

The noise in the kitchen went silent, and almost immediately, I heard the sound of footsteps coming closer. Closing my eyes, I braced myself for the inevitable barrage of questions.

"What?" Jason said when he saw the mess around me. "Clay? What happened?"

I knelt down to pick up the books. "Sorry. It was an accident. I was just... looking for something to read."

Jason waved Patrick back to the kitchen, then started helping me with the books. "Actually," he began to say once we were alone. "There's something I wanted to talk to you about."

"I know," I quickly cut him off as I stacked the books back into place. "You want me to start doing more things."

One of the books slipped out of Jason's hands, but he grabbed it almost before it could hit the floor. "Well, sort of. Patrick and I have been talking, and we think it would be good if you started therapy."

I'd just placed the last of the books I'd picked up back on the shelf, but I nearly knocked them all to the floor again when I spun around to face him. "What? Why? I'm fine."

Jason didn't face me directly, and instead, occupied himself by sorting the books on the shelf back into some sort of order that didn't make any obvious sense.

"No, you're not. Of course you're not. No one would expect you to be fine after... everything."

The only book that didn't make it back onto the shelf was the one I'd initially pulled out. Its weight sat in my hand, pages fanning the air as I gestured with it to emphasize my words. "Oh, and you know how I'm feeling better than I do? I said I'm fine. That means I'm fine."

"Okay." Jason backed up a step, hands held out in front of him. "You're fine. But it would also be okay if you weren't fine. I just think that therapy would be a good idea. You've been through a lot, and therapy can help you process all of it."

The book in my hand was worn around the edges and had obviously been read many times. I tapped the cracked spine against my leg as I ground my teeth against the sudden surge of hot emotion that bubbled up my throat.

"All what?"

"I…" Jason's eyes flickered back and forth, searching my eyes for an answer he couldn't find. "I don't understand."

My hand that wasn't holding the book curled into a fist at my side. "All what? You keep talking about the *things I've been through,* and *everything I've experienced*, but you've never actually said it out loud."

Jason backed up another step, but I followed him.

"I-I don't—" he stuttered, looking everywhere but directly at me.

"What? Can't say it. Fine. I'll say it for you. I was taken. Imprisoned. Raped and tortured. Everyday. For years. And when I finally got free, I chose to go back to doing the exact same thing because that's all I know how to do."

I gripped the book in my hand so hard I could feel the pages bending.

"There. That wasn't so hard to say, was it? Or are you afraid that saying out loud is going to taint your perfect little home."

I had just enough sense not to throw the book directly at him, and instead, hurled it off to the side. My teeth ached from how hard I clenched my jaw, and my whole body shook as I stared into Jason's eyes, watching his emotions fighting each other.

The sound of something breaking was like a slap to the face.

My fury disappeared, evaporating out of existence like a single drop of water landing on the surface of the sun. I practically stopped breathing as I turned to see the book I'd just thrown sitting on the floor, surrounded by a puddle of water and the broken pieces of a glass vase.

Lying on top of it all, like a rose placed on the lid of a coffin, was a single broken orchid stem with its petals scattered across the floor.

I stumbled toward the mess, grasping for the pieces of the broken vase as if I could put it back together.

"I'm sorry. I'm sorry. I didn't mean to."

My hands were shaking so bad, I could barely hold the delicate pieces without dropping them. The vase had once been perfectly clear, but each piece that slipped back to the ground looked a little redder, like it was stained just from my touch.

"Don't touch that!"

Jason grabbed both my wrists in a rough grip and yanked me away from the vase.

I forgot where I was.

I forgot who I was with.

In that moment, as Jason's fingers wrapped around my wrists, all I could see were other hands grabbing me.

Other faces leering at me.

So many unspeakable pains assaulted me at once and I screamed.

"No!"

As soon as it had come, the memory faded, and I was left standing in the middle of a suburban living room, with Jason lying on the floor where he'd fallen after I shoved him.

I ran.

My feet pounded against the stairs as I fled to my room and locked the door behind me. Then the strength left my legs and I collapsed to the floor with my back pressed against the door. I panted for breath, yet I couldn't seem to get any air. My fingers stung when I clawed at my throat, and I left red streaks of blood against my own skin.

I'd cut myself when I'd foolishly tried to pick up broken glass with my bare hands. Jason had only been trying to protect me, and I'd treated him like he was a monster trying to attack me.

Two weeks.

That's all it took for me to fuck it all up.

I was ruining Jason's perfect home. Soon enough, he was going to decide I wasn't worth the trouble and kick me out, assuming he wasn't already packing my bags.

I wrapped my arms around my knees and focused on my breathing. My heart beat a rapid pulse in my ears, drowning out the rest of the world around me. I didn't want to think. I didn't want to feel. I wanted to just stop existing for a while.

Slipping into the Midnight Zone was as easy as breathing at that point. I hovered in the air, looking down at the sad figure of Clay Dahler huddled below me. He created such a pathetic sight, hiding in a bedroom that wasn't really his. I couldn't stand to look at him for long.

So, I left. I rose higher and higher in the air until I was floating among the clouds and the city below me was just a glittering pattern of lights. It was a full moon that night, and I entertained myself dancing between moonbeams as I let the world keep turning without me.

Vibration along my skin dragged me back into my body. I was still in the exact same position, huddled in a ball on the floor, but now someone was knocking on the door behind me. The room was dark, giving no indication of the time. I was pretty sure it was the same day, but other than that, time was meaningless.

"Clay?" Jason spoke from the other side of the door.

I tried to respond, but my throat was constricted, and I couldn't make more than a strange croaking sound.

That seemed to be enough for Jason, however, because he kept talking as if I'd answered him properly.

"I'm sorry. I shouldn't have grabbed you like that. I just didn't want you to get hurt. And... you're right. I have been avoiding talking about... about how those monsters hurt you. I just didn't know what to say."

He sighed, and there was a thump against the door that sounded suspiciously like a human skull hitting wood.

"I'm fucking this up, and I feel like no matter what I do I'm just going to make it worse. So... here."

Something slipped under the door, and I picked it up to find it was Jason's phone. The screen showed a video call already in progress, and Logan's face stared up at me.

"You don't trust me," Jason explained. "I had hoped... well, that doesn't matter. I noticed that you did seem to trust Logan, so maybe he can help where I can't."

The sound of footsteps leading away from the door followed his words, and I realized he'd left.

Part of me felt extremely guilty for making my brother worry so much, but I was also so relieved to see Logan that I couldn't concentrate on anything else. I'd missed him a lot more than I realized, and my fingers shook as I unmuted the video call.

"Hey, Clay," Logan's voice greeted me through the phone. "How're you doing?"

All at once, I explained everything that happened that evening in one long ramble. I barely stopped to take a breath as the words poured out of me. I even tried to describe the flashback memory I'd experienced when Jason grabbed me. My description probably didn't make much sense, but I trusted that Logan would understand anyway.

"Flashbacks like that are common," he assured me when I was done.

"But, why? I'm safe now. Those memories shouldn't matter anymore."

"It's because you're safe that your mind is trying to process those memories. Your brother is right. Therapy would help."

"I'm not crazy."

Logan quickly cut me off. "I'm not saying you're crazy. That's not what therapy is about. I'm not even saying you have to do it. That's your decision in the end. But I'm going to send over a list of resources that might help you, and I'd like you to at least consider them. All right?"

I scowled, but I didn't have the energy to keep protesting. "Fine. I'm sick of talking about this now. Talk about something else."

He thought for a moment, and even through the small screen, I could see the way his cheeks dimpled when he pursed his lips. For most people, dimples were attached to smiles, but Logan smiled so much that his dimples only appeared when he was deep in thought.

"I recently started listening to Tibetan flute music."

I snorted. "Tibetan flute music? Really?"

"Hey, don't knock it. It's pretty good."

We spent several hours talking about different things, from music, to movies, and even the books I'd tried reading. In all that time, we never came back to the topic of my most recent panic attack or the suggestion of therapy.

Yet, when I finally ended the call, I found myself seriously considering it with a more open mind.

Maybe therapy wasn't such a bad idea.

CHAPTER FOURTEEN

Logan

MY SECOND TRIP to San Francisco felt significantly shorter than the first time, despite it being the same number of miles. Less than a day after I crossed the border into the city for a second time, I found myself sitting in a random, rundown diner with a familiar young man sitting beside me.

I'd only met Jordy once for a few minutes, and I'd feared he would be hard to find again. Yet, like the pull of an invisible compass arrow, my steps drew me right to the same abandoned archway where I'd met him the first time. He was there, still huddled against the wall, as if he'd been waiting for me all that time.

Steam rose from the bowl cupped in Jordy's hands, which hovered like a cloud before his face.

"Doorbell cameras."

The spoon I'd been idly stirring around my coffee cup clinked heavily against the side, echoing in the mostly empty dinner.

"What?"

Jordy didn't look at me and stared vacantly into the steam. "You said Clay told you about how the Bell ringers operate. Well, he doesn't know this, about a year after they let him go, they started using a new tactic. You know those home security systems with doorbell cameras? I'm not sure how, but they've managed to get access to some of the systems that support those cameras. They used to find victims by ringing doorbells, but now they're in the doorbells."

This information should have surprised me, but it didn't. These "Bell ringers" already snatched children right out of their homes. To them, using the very systems that were supposed to keep kids safe as a way to prey on them was probably just a matter of efficiency.

"Are the security companies involved, or are they unaware that someone is tapping into their systems?"

Jordy shrugged and took another sip of his soup, drinking straight from the bowl and not even bothering to use the spoon provided. "I don't know. Could be some of both. I don't really know how those things work. I don't even have a smartphone that can download apps. Just a cheap flip-phone for calls and texts. You'll have to ask someone who knows more about these things."

At the mention of smartphone, I was reminded to pull out my own phone and start making notes about this new information.

"Doorbell cameras. I hadn't thought to look at something like that. We've been checking into other door-to-door services, and we've managed to find a few new cases of missing kids that we think are related. This new angle should help a lot. Thanks."

With a few decisive nods, like he was psyching himself up, Jordy finished off the last of his soup then jumped up from the stool he was sitting on.

"All right. Let's do this before I lose my

nerve.”

After paying, I led him out of the diner to the building across the street. It was a facility that specialized in recovery for trafficking victims. Not every city, or even every state, was lucky enough to have these kinds of places, so I was glad to find one so close to home for Jordy.

“I’ve called ahead,” I assured him as we hesitated in front of the doors. “They know to expect you. And you have my number. If there’s anything wrong, you aren’t comfortable here or you don’t think they can help you, then just call me. Any time.”

Jordy’s blue eyes were wide as he stared up at the sign. Whatever thought or memory that was playing in his mind utterly consumed him, and I wasn’t even sure if he could see the building standing in front of him.

One of his hands drifted over to clutch his inner forearm.

“You know... I’m lucky. A lot of the other kids never made it out, and those that did were so hooked on hard drugs that they didn’t survive for long. The fact that I’m here, and I’m mostly clean... I have Clay to thank for that.”

The moment Clay's name was mentioned, I was hanging on Jordy's every word. Not wanting to seem too eager, I tried to keep my tone casual as I asked him what he meant, but on the inside, I was vibrating with the need for him to keep speaking.

I may as well have not bothered. He barely noticed me, he was so lost in his own thoughts. "Clay was smart. He never fought them or gave them an excuse to drug him. Even the ones that hurt us and wanted us to fight. He only gave them what they wanted, and nothing more. Kids who fought too much were drugged, or worse, they disappeared. Clay knew how to make them feel like they were the ones in control. It was why they let him go in the end. He wasn't a threat to them. I copied his example, acted exactly as he did, and I was able to escape, too."

The light returned to his eyes and he focused on me again.

"You're still in contact with Clay, right? Is he doing okay with his brother?"

I thought back to the brothers' tearful first meeting, along with every phone and video call I'd exchanged with Clay since then. Nearly a month had passed since I'd taken Clay to Maryland. Things had been rocky between the brothers at first, but their relationship seemed to be improving.

"It hasn't been an easy adjustment for him, but he's moving in the right direction and taking the time to heal."

"That's good." Jordy nodded one last time. "Keep taking care of him. I owe him a lot, even if he doesn't realize it."

That was a promise I didn't even need to make, but I did. Jordy looked more comforted by my promise to help Clay than by my promise to help him. As I led Jordy inside the building, I wondered how deeply his decision to follow Clay's example really ran.

If my suspicions were correct, more than one life depended on Clay's success.

CHAPTER FIFTEEN

Logan

IT WAS NEARLY midnight when I finally stepped through the door of my own apartment and collapsed on my bed.

After dropping Clay off in Maryland a month ago, I'd returned to Baton Rouge to immediately pull the newly named "Bell ringer" case back off the shelf. Roland was assisting in the case, and Sebastian and Damien lent a hand whenever they could, but overall, it had been one long night after another.

Add in my little impromptu trip back to San Francisco to find Jordy and repay him for helping me, and I hadn't seen the inside of my own apartment very much since I left Clay behind.

No.

I didn't leave him behind.

I returned him to his brother, his family, where he belonged.

I'd repeated this mantra to myself so many times over the last month that it almost felt true, but I still couldn't shake the lingering sense of guilt whispering in my ear that I had abandoned him.

As if the very universe were laughing at me, my phone rang with a familiar ringtone.

Clay was calling me.

Nothing could have stopped my finger from hitting the "answer" button.

A video call popped up on the screen. He hated talking on the phone without being able to see who he was talking to, so Clay almost exclusively used video calls. In the split second before the video opened, I sat up in a more presentable posture so my exhaustion wouldn't be so evident.

"Clay," I greeted with a cheerful voice that only felt a little forced. "What's up? How're things going?"

"All right," Clay said with a distracted

tone. Even looking at him on such a small screen, I could see him fidgeting. Based on the background behind him, it looked like he was in his bedroom, sitting near the window. The hand not holding the phone kept opening and closing the blinds. The orange glow from the streetlight outside would illuminate the room just long enough for me to see all of Clay's face, then it would disappear and cast the image on the screen back into the gray haze of twilight.

I wanted Clay to elaborate, or even explain why he'd called, but he didn't say anything more as he continued to play with the blinds.

"Have you gotten your results back from the doctor, yet?" I asked. It was one of the more pertinent questions that had been hanging on my mind. He hadn't been to a proper doctor since he was kidnapped. Even without any other factors, that alone was enough for him to need a doctor's checkup. Plus, there was no telling what he might have been exposed to in the years since then.

Clay sighed and his shoulders slumped back into a more natural posture, like he was relieved that I'd started the conversation for him.

"I'm fine. Nothing to worry about. The one thing my captors did teach me was how to look after my health. Farmers don't want their cattle getting sick, after all."

He laughed, but I just scowled at him.

"Clay."

He immediately waved me off. "Yeah. Yeah. Self-depreciation and deflecting with humor aren't healthy communication. I know."

He was clearly quoting something that he had heard many times before, and although he looked annoyed, I couldn't help but smile.

"It sounds like you've had your first therapy appointment. How'd it go?"

Clay shrugged and went back to playing with the blinds. "First two appointments, actually. I'll be going three times a week for a while, until I'm more stable."

He rolled his eyes so hard on the word 'stable' that I was surprised he didn't fall right out the open window.

"So? Was it as bad as you feared?"

I meant for the joke to lighten the mood and maybe finally bring a smile to his face. However, Clay's fidgeting grew even more manic, and he looked away from the screen.

"Logan. Have you ever attended therapy before?"

"A couple of times."

My easy answer seemed to surprise him, and he looked back at the screen like I'd just illuminated the light at the end of a long, dark tunnel.

"When? What was it like?"

Since this was gearing up to be a long conversation, I moved over to the comfortable armchair near my bed and propped the phone up against a couple of books. "The first time was right after I got out of the Air Force. I'd seen other people I served with struggle to make the adjustment back to civilian life, and I didn't want to follow in their footsteps. The second time..." I hesitated.

Would my answer hit too close to home and upset Clay, or would it bring him comfort?

Either was a possibility.

Deciding to take the risk, I answered honestly.

"The second time was after some undercover work I did a few years ago.

Working for the bad guys, even if it was just pretend, messed with my head for a while. Why do you ask?"

Clay must have propped his own phone up on something, because I could now see both of his hands in the frame of the screen, twisting around each other like he meant to tie his fingers into knots.

"Was it... I mean... How did it make you feel?"

I grimaced, and my exaggerated expression managed to earn a small chuckle from Clay. "It wasn't fun. Kinda feels like dissecting your own brain, and you often don't like what you find, but overall, it helped in the end. Why? How does it make you feel?"

That must have been what was weighing on Clay. The moment I asked the question, he immediately stopped fidgeting and fell deathly still instead.

"I don't like it," he said in a small voice, almost whispering. "It makes me feel..." He shook his head, and his shoulders slumped until he looked even smaller on the screen. "I don't want to go back. It isn't going to help."

Running my hand though my hair, I took a moment to choose my words carefully. "Therapy isn't an immediate cure. It takes time. The mind is tricky. Isn't like a broken leg that you can heal just by slapping a cast on it. You're going to have to dig up a lot of painful things in order to figure out how to heal them, and that can feel really bad at first. But I promise, it will be worth it in the end."

My hopes of reassuring him were dashed as I watched him curl up on the window seat until his arms were wrapped around his knees. It was exactly the same position I'd found him in when I barged into his apartment in San Francisco.

"I told Jason I didn't want to go back, and we fought about it. He said the same thing."

Not for the first time, I hated the miles between Maryland and Louisiana. I wanted nothing more than to reach out to him, but the distance made that impossible. If he were even a single state over, I probably would have gotten in my car and driven to him that night. However, seven states were a much harder obstacle to overcome.

"Look..." I sighed again. "Neither Jason nor I can make you do something you don't want to do. But—"

There wasn't even time for me to try and make an argument before he cut me off.

"I do want to do it. I want to get better. I want to finally feel okay in my own head, and I don't mind if the process is difficult or painful. I just don't want to have to relive the details over and over. I've already lived through it all, once. I can't do it again."

"Wait a minute..." I instinctively held up my hand to cut off his rambling, even though I couldn't actually reach him from so far away. "You've only been to two appointments, right? What kind of details would you be getting into already?"

"Everything," Clay practically exploded. "This guy, Doctor... whatever his name is. He wants to know details about everything. Like... okay, so, we were talking about when I was kidnapped. And I thought that made sense because that's where it all started. But then we got into the first time I was made to... you know, do anything. And this doctor guy kept asking about what they made me do and how they made me do it. When I tried to just give a vague answer, he insisted that I had to describe things in detail. He said

I'd never heal if I didn't face the reality of what happened to me, but I have faced it. I faced it every day, for years. Why do I have to relive these things again? This doesn't feel like it's helping me. It feels like..."

The energy of his sudden outburst drained away like someone had pulled a plug inside him and emptied him out. I half expected to see him deflate like a balloon as he wrapped his arms around his knees again.

"It feels like I'm catering to another client, only this time I'm the one paying."

On the surface, Clay's description of his therapy sessions sounded inappropriate. The protective side of me was tempted to storm back off to the other side of the country and demand that therapist have his license revoked.

However, Clay wasn't the first victim of sexual violence that I'd dealt with. I'd seen firsthand how people dealing with his kind of trauma could misinterpret innocent situations and twist them into threats. As much as I wanted to just believe him, I couldn't trust his mental state enough to take his description at face value.

That didn't mean I was going to disregard his concerns. Whether the therapist was actually being inappropriate or not, there was something we needed to do either way.

"I think you need to change to a different therapist, Clay. Maybe this therapist has honest intentions. Maybe he doesn't. I promise, I'll look into it. However, I do know that therapy works a lot better if you're comfortable with the therapist, which you clearly aren't. So, how about this... I'll call your brother, and we'll see about getting you moved to a different therapist. I don't know the therapists in your area, but I can probably call around and get some recommendations. If we do manage to find a therapist that you're comfortable with, will you promise to give it another try and stick with it for a while?"

Clay agreed, but the mood of the conversation had definitely soured. Not wanting to leave on such a negative note, I asked him to tell me about something fun that he'd done recently.

At first, he looked hesitant, but then his gaze landed on something just off screen, and his eyes lit up.

"Oh, yeah." He grabbed several books and held them up in front of the camera. "So, Jason and Patrick have a bunch of books in the house, but Patrick noticed I wasn't enjoying them, so he took me to the bookstore to pick out some for myself. I wasn't sure what to think of him at first, but he's a pretty nice guy. Like an actually nice guy, you know. Not one of those self-proclaimed *Nice Guys*."

I nodded along, happy that Clay had found something to enjoy, but then I read the titles of the books he was showing me.

Goosebumps.

Anamorphs.

A Wrinkle in Time.

They were all books I'd read in middle school, and while there was nothing wrong with adults enjoying books meant for a younger audience, the fact that Clay had exclusively picked out those titles worried me.

Clay must have noticed my expression, because he pulled the books back to his chest and laughed nervously. "Yeah. I haven't attended school since I was thirteen and didn't really have the chance to keep up with my education. Turns out, I'm a bit behind when it comes to reading skills. Patrick had me take some sort of online test to figure out where I'm at, and he said that these books would be better for me. He also said that I just need practice, and even mentioned that I could get a tutor if I wanted, and maybe take the GED someday."

I wanted to kick myself.

How had I not considered the greater impact that being kidnapped at the age of fourteen would have on his life?

Of course he was reading kid's books. He'd missed the opportunity to read them as an actual kid. In a way, it was like his entire life had been put on pause almost a decade ago, and now he was trying to pick it back up from where he left off.

My silence lasted too long as I struggled through my self-criticizing thoughts and Clay began to grow visibly uncomfortable. He laughed again, rubbing at the back of his head as blue eyes peeked at me from under his bangs.

"Is, um... is Patrick right? Do I just need to practice? These books are a lot easier to read than the adult books, but I'd like to read adult books too someday."

Snapping out of my own thoughts, I scoffed and waved a dismissive hand.

"Psh. A lot of adult books are boring. Don't get too hung up on them. You should read what you like."

My reaction was a little too over the top to be natural, but Clay seemed to appreciate it, nonetheless.

Casting my memories back to my middle school days, I recalled the few Goosebumps books that I had read and told Clay about my favorites. One of them turned out to be the same that he bought, and he ended up reading the first chapter to me over the video call.

We both pretended that it was for the sake of helping him practice, but in reality, it was just an excuse. Neither of us wanted to end the call yet, and we ended up talking into the early hours of the morning.

I was going to be dead tired at work tomorrow, but it was worth it as I watched Clay focusing on the page in front of him, reading to me with a small smile on his face.

CHAPTER SIXTEEN

Logan

"YOU GO AROUND looking like that, people are going to think you lost a fight."

Sebastian's voice greeted me with far too much enthusiasm when I stepped through the door of Alias Investigations.

I wanted to flip him off and tell him to shove his laughter up his ass, but I was too tired and just slumped into the chair on the other side of his desk.

"Shut up. I just didn't get enough sleep last night."

"You sure it was only one night?" Sebastian eyed me up and down, laughter still evident in his voice, though his expression conveyed legitimate worry. "I've seen raccoons with smaller dark circles around their eyes than you have right now. I think you're missing more than a single night's sleep."

"I'll be fine. It's just been a busy couple of weeks. Now, what did you want to talk to me about?"

As I'd predicted, work had been hell when I was practically falling asleep on my feet. I'd been banned from any fieldwork that day and spent the time catching up on paperwork. When it was done, I'd been looking forward to falling into my bed and not moving for the next twelve hours, but a last-minute call from Sebastian had derailed that plan.

A file sat on the desk, obviously waiting for me, but when I reached for it, Sebastian pulled it away.

"Hey, Logan, maybe you should just go home and rest. We can discuss this later."

"Sebastian." I slammed my fist against the top of the desk, though my display of anger lost its impact when I was also slumped over that same desk. "I'm already here. Just give it to me."

Sebastian—the annoying bastard—chuckled as he opened the file. "Didn't know you were so forward, Logan. Usually, I have to buy someone dinner before they'll beg me like that."

I glared at the other man, wishing I had the energy to throw something at his stupid, smug face.

My prayers were answered when a paperback book came sailing out of nowhere and bounced off the side of Sebastian's head.

Gabe strode into the room a moment later, glaring at Sebastian as he returned the book. "If you're cheating on Newt, I will break that leg of yours beyond repair this time."

The intense look in his eyes meant business, and I half expected him to reach over and break Sebastian's leg right in front of me.

Sebastian, on the other hand, just laughed harder.

"Don't look so worried, Logan. I promise, Gabe may lack a sense of humor, but he's not as mean as he seems." Then his laughter died and was replaced with a serious expression as he turned in his chair to face Gabe directly. "I promise I'm not cheating on Newt. So, you can stop plotting my murder."

Gabe's expression barely changed, but he gave Sebastian a slight nod as he moved over to his own desk. "Good. I don't want to explain to Frankie why his best friend's boyfriend is in the hospital again."

Sebastian leaned over the side of his desk, getting as close as he could to Gabe's space without standing up. The shit-eating grin was back on his face, stronger than before.

"Hospital? So, you wouldn't kill me and put me directly in the morgue? I'm flattered."

Gabe merely scoffed and started checking the book he'd used as a projectile for damage.

I hadn't noticed while it was flying through the air, but based on the cover, the book seemed to be a sappy romance novel. From how much Gabe was worrying over the book, it was obviously his, but I never would have expected such a serious man to like those kinds of stories.

Maybe Sebastian was right, and Gabe wasn't as cold-hearted as he looked. In fact, the more I studied him, the more I began to suspect he was truly a romantic at heart who just took his relationships very seriously.

That was a quality I could appreciate in a man. Gabe wasn't my type at all, but I could see how he could make the right person very happy.

Speaking of which...

"Newt? Frankie? These are new names. Something you want to tell me?"

"Oh." Sebastian perked up and immediately pulled out his phone. "Did I not tell you? My bachelor days are in the past. Here."

The photo on the phone showed Sebastian standing with his arm around another man. The little redhead, who I assumed was named Newt, couldn't be more different from Sebastian if he tried. While Sebastian was dressed in a long black coat like he was auditioning for a Matrix reboot, Newt was dressed in as many colors as possible. The two of them seemed to be at a convention or fair of some sort and were posing for the picture with comically serious expressions on their faces while holding up peace signs toward the camera.

"You look good together," I said as I handed back the phone. I meant it, too.

Although they were very different, they also somehow complimented each other. Like black and white, a picture needed both in order to create an image. Remove one, and you'd be left with just a blank piece of paper.

"Yeah." Sebastian smiled down at the phone before putting it away. "Our relationship had an interesting start. He got wrapped up in the case with the pedophile ring. Nearly got killed when Russo's goons struck a hit on me at the old office and apartment, too, but he stuck it out like a trooper. Now, I think we're in a pretty good place."

He leaned across the desk toward me, cupping his hand in front of his mouth to stage whisper at me while blatantly staring over at Gabe.

"Newt's best friend, Frankie, is also dating Gabe. Two of us are practically in-laws now, so I've got to be on my best behavior."

Ah, that made sense. I'd known Sebastian Roth for several years, and he usually wasn't the type to let new people into his inner circle so easily. At first, despite being vetted by Mason, I'd been suspicious of how quickly Gabe had been integrated into Sebastian's life, but with this extra tie between them, the relationship made more sense.

I was happy to see my friend thriving, especially after the difficulties he'd faced recently, but it was a bittersweet feeling. It wasn't jealousy, exactly, that sat heavy in my stomach. Sebastian's partner, Newt, wasn't my type any more than Gabe was. I'd always preferred men with a bit more spice to them in both looks and personality.

Yet, I was jealous of his relationship. I couldn't remember the last time I'd managed more than a few dates with the same person, and I longed for the stability of knowing there would always be someone waiting for me when I came home.

Clearing my throat to drive away the ball of emotion that had decided to form there, I tapped the folder that was still lying on the desk.

"You said you had something to tell me? I assuming it wasn't just about your relationship."

"Ah, right." Sebastian flipped open the folder and we were finally able to get to work. "Until now, we've been operating under the assumption that our two cases were unconnected."

"Yeah," I agreed as I looked through the information in the file. It was mostly a lot of names and numbers that didn't make much sense without context, so I don't bother to look for long. "Although both trafficking rings prey on kids, their victims and methods are completely different. Why? Has something changed?"

Sebastian's previously cheerful expression grew pensive as he braced his elbows on the desk and laced his fingers in front of his face. "I don't know if something has changed, or if we just didn't have all the information before. Until now, these "Bell ringers" seemed old school. Going door-to-door. Physically stalking victims. Snatching them out of their houses in the dead of night. Those are tactics from a pre-technology era. The traffickers we've been chasing, in contrast, are very-high tech. Altering records. Manipulating systems. That kinda stuff."

In a sudden burst of clarity, I realized what he was saying.

"The doorbell cameras."

Sebastian nodded and a chilling

shadow fell over his eyes. "When you told me about the info that Jordy gave you, I started to wonder. That's a high-tech tactic that would require a lot of manpower and a lot of technological know-how."

"Which sounds exactly how the traffickers you've been hunting down operate," I concluded for him. "You think they're the same people?"

Sebastian idly sorted the information back inside the file, straightening the pages until they were perfectly aligned.

"I hope I'm wrong, or that your *Bell ringers* are just an extension of the ring Gabe and I brought down that we didn't catch. But..."

He sighed and slumped behind his desk. Those few words seemed to have taken all his energy to say, and he wasn't done.

I could already see the connection he was making, so to save him the effort, I finished the explanation for him.

"You think the ring I'm hunting and the ring you're hunting are both just branches on a much larger tree."

Taking a deep breath and running both hands through his hair, Sebastian straightened his spine and forced a grin back onto his face.

"Well, maybe I'm wrong. Hell, I wouldn't be surprised if I'm just jumping at shadows and seeing threats where they aren't. This case has driven me half crazy."

The hair stood up on the back of my neck. Sebastian's words sounded suspiciously similar to what I'd been thinking about Clay last night. I'd managed to make a few calls today to find out more about the therapist he was visiting, and so far, I didn't like what I'd found. I still couldn't say for certain that the doctor was being inappropriate with his patients, but it was enough to raise my suspicions. I'd already arranged with Clay's brother to have him moved to a different therapist.

If Sebastian's instincts were as accurate as Clay's had been, then we couldn't afford to ignore his ideas just because they were uncomfortable.

"Tell me everything about your case. From the beginning."

CHAPTER SEVENTEEN

Logan

THE BODY LYING beneath me was warm and inviting. I buried my face against their neck, feeling the rapid pulse beating against my mouth, and drowning myself in the scent of moonlight, chocolate, and raw desire.

My hand tangled in mid-length hair, tugging at it just hard enough to make the other person moan.

Wait.

I knew that voice.

I pulled back and braced myself on my hands to stare down into familiar blue eyes.

"Clay?"

With the same inviting smile that he'd used when we first met in a San Francisco hotel room, Clay called my name and wrapped his arms around my neck. A thought floated through my mind that I should push him away.

This couldn't be right.

How was he even here?

Yet, I remained frozen as he pulled me closer. Our lips touched and my restraint crumbled.

I fell into him...

...and woke up gasping among the sweaty tangled sheet of my own bed. The room spun. In the darkness, I swore I could still see Clay's face looking up at me, making my heart race even after the dream had ended.

One hand hesitantly trailed down my stomach to grip the waistband of my boxers and lift them just enough for me to confirm my suspicions. Evidence of my wet dream stained my thighs and the inside of my boxers, already cooling against my heated skin.

Letting the waistband snap back into place, I collapsed back against my pillow.

"Fuck."

CHAPTER EIGHTEEN

Clay

SOMEONE WAS STARING at me.

I could feel their eyes, and although it wasn't threatening, it also wasn't pleasant.

As I set up the board games in the communal area, I kept my head down and tried to focus on the work, choosing games that required the most set up in order to keep myself busy.

It had been a year since I came to back Maryland and after each of the seasons had their turn, summer had rolled around again. A lot had changed, but at the same time things also stayed the same.

I'd gone through several different therapists over the year. None of them were as bad as the first—according to rumors, the man had his license revoked—but it had taken me two more therapists after him before I finally found one that I was comfortable with. Doctor Coleman was a motherly woman, but in a no-nonsense way that didn't take any shit or tolerate any disrespect. I liked it, as it felt more familiar and comforting than the people who tried to coddle me or treat me too gently. Yet, she never went too far or stepped over the line while she was pushing me to better myself, and her efforts seemed to be paying off.

About four months after starting therapy, I'd picked up some volunteer work at a local halfway house for homeless kids. It was technically open to anyone in need, but the number of LGBTQ+ kids who sheltered at the halfway house was staggeringly high, and a lot of them had faced abuse in some way.

At first, I'd worried that seeing so many people with similar stories to mine would cause me to relapse, but I actually found it cathartic. Like facing my demons head on.

My presence there also seemed to give the kids hope that things could get better.

Well, I called them kids, but most of them were only a few years younger than me.

Leslie, one of the other volunteers, stepped up to my side. We weren't exactly friends, but we were friendly in the way that people who regularly worked together were. She had once taken shelter at the halfway house, and now that she was older and able to support herself, she was returning the favor by volunteering.

She waited for a moment until she was sure I recognized her, before bumping my shoulder. "Looks like someone has a crush."

"What?"

She nodded in another direction with her chin. I followed her gaze and found the source of the stare I'd felt earlier. A young man was watching me from the other side of the room, but when he realized I'd noticed him, he quickly looked away.

"What's his problem?"

Leslie snorted and pushed her round glasses back up her nose when they slid down. "Really? Come on, Clay. He's obviously smitten with you. Kenneth never used to attend game night, or any other group activity, really. But since you started volunteering here, he's always the first to sign up."

I scowled at her. I wasn't angry, but I was confused, and that usually brought a whole host of other negative emotions.

"Okaaaay. But, like, isn't that inappropriate? He's one of the kids."

"Not really. He is one of the older ones that are still here. I think he turns twenty next month. That's only three years younger than you."

"Four years," I reminded her. "I turned twenty-four a little while ago." That wasn't the point and we both knew it. Three years or four years made no difference, but I was still trying to get my head around what Leslie was saying. "Okay. So, he's not a kid. That still doesn't explain what you expect me to do about it?

Leslie just shrugged and finished setting up the monopoly game board that I had abandoned. "Well, you could talk to him. Or you could continue to ignore him. It's up to you and what you feel comfortable with. There isn't really a right or wrong answer here."

Before I could answer, Dominic's ear-catching voice announced the start of the game night and directed everyone to find a seat.

Dominic O'Connor owned the halfway house. He was a large man with an equally boisterous personality. Sometimes so much so that it seemed forced. A middle-aged gut protruded slightly over his belt, but was disguised by his well-tailored clothes, and his thick hair looked like it had never known a split end in its life. Overall, he seemed like the kind of person who'd never known hardship a day in his life, though I had long learned not to be deceived by appearances.

When I'd first met him, I'd been suspicious. A man who surrounded himself with vulnerable kids must have bad intentions, and I'd been hypercritical of every word he said, looking for the signs of a predator.

Yet, my suspicions had slid right off him as if he was Teflon, and he never got upset over my behavior or accusations. Eventually, with the help of Doctor Coleman, I'd learned how to separate my own life experiences from reality and see what was in front of me rather than what I expected. When I did that, I found that Dominic was as genuine as he presented himself, and really just wanted to help as many people as he could.

As I'd eventually found out, my initial thoughts about him couldn't have been more wrong. Once he got to know you, there'd be times where his façade slipped and the history of his great loss was evident in his face. There was compassion in his eyes that could only be earned through hard life experiences. The loss of his son was his motivator in all that he did now.

We needed more people like Dominic in the world.

It was ironic, if you thought about it. If everyone in the world was like Dominic, then Dominic wouldn't have been needed, because the halfway house would be empty.

When I wasn't volunteering at Dominic's place or going to one of my regular therapy sessions—which had dropped down from thrice a week to only twice—I held down a laughable job at Jason's construction company.

It could barely be called a job. I knew nothing about construction, so I couldn't help with the actual work. Instead, Jason had hired me as the company's unofficial secretary.

Well, it was official. I had an employment record and everything. I only called it unofficial because it was obvious my brother wasn't giving me the workload of an actual secretary. The company already had an actual secretary who handled most things, and anyone could see my workload did not match hers.

I came in for a few hours four times a week, filed paperwork, answered phone calls, and overall, just tried to make myself useful. In return, I earned a full-time salary, with benefits. I would have protested being given such a lucrative job out of pity, but Jason's charity was the only way I was going to get any experience to start building a resume, and half my earnings went back to him as rent anyway.

That was the one thing I'd insisted on. At first, he'd refused my offer to pay rent, but he'd been forced to give in when I started hiding the cash in places where he could find it, like under his pillow or in the cup holder in his car.

Jason's most recent jobsite was just a few blocks down the street from the halfway house. The building they were constructing would eventually be a series of low rent apartments that would also be owned by Dominic. It was meant to be like a part two of his grand plan. Kids from the halfway house, once they reached adulthood, would need a place to stay, and there would always be apartments available for them. This would actually be the second of its kind that Dominic had commissioned; the first one being after his son was killed several years ago.

The building was currently only half done, and currently stood as a skeleton of its final design. It was too bad it wasn't finished yet. There were several people still living at the halfway house who were already technically too old. Kenneth was almost twenty and had avoided homelessness only because Dominic was too kind to kick anyone out. He could definitely use one of the apartments currently being built.

Summer had just started, so Maryland's seasonal rainstorms hadn't quite started yet. The dug-up ground around the temporary office was still dry, so I didn't have to stomp my way to the door like I had to do on wetter days, and I breathed a sigh of relief when I stepped into the office still as clean as when I left the halfway house.

"Hey, Clay," Jason greeted me when I stepped through the door without looking up from his paperwork. "You're back early. How was the halfway house?"

"Same as usual."

I thought my tone was normal as I took a seat behind the designated secretary desk on the other side of the little room, but Jason must have picked up on something in my voice, because he immediately put down his paperwork and looked at me with a furrowed brow.

"What's wrong? You're usually eager to talk about your volunteer work."

Sitting on the desk was a kinetic statue that used magnets to keep itself perpetually spinning. I'd never bought it, and no one else claimed to have brought it in either. It seemed to be one of those things that just naturally spawned in an office environment.

Staring at the jumble of metallic spheres and rods, I tapped one of the pieces and sent the whole thing spinning.

"What do you think about dating?"

His gaze briefly flicked to the ring on his left hand. "I think I'm married, so it's not really an appropriate thing for me to be doing any more."

"I don't mean you," I quickly corrected him.

"Oh." He paused for a moment, and then his eyes lit up. "Oooooh. You mean, like, what do I think about *you* dating?"

"You don't have to say it like it's such a surprise," I grumbled.

Jason blushed and looked sheepish, but I was already chastising myself in my head. He hadn't said anything wrong.

Why was I being so hostile?

"Sorry," Jason muttered as he rearranged the paperwork on his desk, moving things around only to put them right back in the same spot. "I didn't think. It hasn't come up before, so I guess I just assumed you weren't interested or weren't ready for that kind of stuff."

I slumped against the desk and caught the little kinetic statue, so it stopped spinning. "I don't know if I am, but it came up and you're the only one I know who has actually won the dating game, so

I was wondering what you thought about it."

Jason glanced at his wedding ring again, this time flashing me with a bright smile. "I did win the dating game. Didn't I."

I made a fake gagging sound, mocking him for being so mushy. In response, he pelted me with several paperclips.

"Hey, don't mock me. You'll understand it someday. When you find the person, you click with, you're gonna want to be all mushy, too. Just you wait."

I scoffed again, but I couldn't ignore the little flame of hope that lit inside me.

Would I ever be like that with someone?

It sounded nice, but I couldn't imagine it. I already struggled to trust people and marrying someone required trust that bordered on blind faith. Even if I did find someone I felt that way about, certainly no one would feel that way about me.

Jason and Patrick were the cliché that everyone secretly aspired for. High school sweethearts who beat the odds and stayed together through college to eventually get married. They were proud of the fact that they'd been each other's firsts and wore it like a badge of honor.

I couldn't even remember who'd been my first. I'd been unconscious for most of it.

No.

No one would look at me with the same kind of pure love that Jason and Patrick shared.

Physical attraction?

Sure. I was practically the master of that. Especially now that I was living in better conditions, eating regularly, and could afford all the hygiene products I wanted. My looks were more stunning than ever. I had no shame admitting that much.

But that beauty was surface deep. Underneath the outer layer, I was still an ugly, broken thing, and although I was healing, some scars would never go away.

I'd lost the opportunity to be marriage material.

Another paperclip bounced off my forehead, hitting me right between the eyes.

"Hey." I rubbed my forehead and scowled at Jason. "What was that for?"

"For thinking too much," Jason said, before throwing another paperclip, which

I snatched out of the air before it could land. "I can practically see your brain spinning from here, and that usually means you're criticizing yourself. So, stop it."

I pouted and scooped up the paperclips that now littered my desk. At first, I meant to store them in the desk drawer, but one of them had accidentally magnetized to the kinetic statue on the desk and stuck straight out like a cactus spike. One by one, I added the other paperclips as well, turning the entire sculpture thorny.

"I'm not criticizing myself," I said as I decided where to place the next paperclip. "I'm just... evaluating my options. Even if I did want to start dating, there aren't many opportunities for me, so what's the point?"

Jason tossed me more paperclips, no longer throwing them at me as punishment, but instead helping to fuel my artistic endeavors. "The point is practice. Just like with reading, you need to start small and work your way up, so you learn how to be in a relationship. You don't need to date someone and immediately want to marry someone."

Over the last year, my reading had gotten better. I'd progressed from a middle-grade level to a high school level. That was still behind where I should be, but it was progress.

Nearly the entire sculpture was now covered in paperclips, making it look like it was covered in metallic fur. If I sent the structure spinning now, the paperclips would be thrown around the room like confetti.

"You married the first person you dated."

"But I didn't know I was going to marry Patrick when I first met him. I just got lucky."

I snorted, blowing my blond bangs out of my face. My hair was long enough to tie back now, so long as I made the world's smallest ponytail, but I usually let it hang free.

"Luck has never been on my side."

I didn't have to look to know that Jason was scowling at me from across the room.

"That's not the point. I'm saying you don't have to think about it so hard. Date, or don't date. It's up to you. But don't shy away from it just because you don't know what you want yet. The point isn't to know what you're looking for. The point is to look."

I hovered my hand over the kinetic statue, inches away from sending the whole thing spinning and making a mess. It would be satisfying to watch the chaos unfold as paperclips went flying everywhere.

But then I'd have to spend the next hour crawling around on the floor picking everything up. The momentary joy I'd get wasn't worth the amount of work it would cost me later.

I returned my hand to my desk, and then rested my head on my crossed arms. On the other side of the room, Jason returned to his paperwork. I watched him, mentally prodding at my sense of guilt the same way one would rub at a bruise to feel the ache. I should be doing my job and helping with the business. Not sitting here moping about the tragedy of my dating life.

Without meaning to, I dozed off. I only worked a few hours at a time, so my nap ended up consuming my entire workday.

When pay for that workday ended up in my bank account anyway, I tried to insist Jason take it back, but he refused, and I eventually gave up.

What I'd come to learn in the last year was that my brother was usually right, and this time was no different.

CHAPTER NINETEEN

Clay

IT HAD STARTED to rain again. The dry weather couldn't hold out forever, and when the rains returned, they came back with a vengeance as if making up for lost time. Like a silver curtain covering the world, I couldn't see more than a few feet beyond the awning where I was taking cover.

What in the world had possessed me to agree to this?

Jason's words about dating and practice had stuck in my head, and before I knew it, I had agreed to go on a date with Kenneth.

It had been surprisingly easy. The next time I'd been at the halfway house, and I'd ended up speaking with Kenneth, all I had to do was wait for him to start hinting again and agree. From there, we decided on a day and time to meet, and that was that.

I'd had "meetings" with clients that were harder to arrange.

My first moment of real doubt came as I waited outside the movie theater by myself, peering through the heavy rain for a hint of Kenneth approaching.

What if he changed his mind and didn't show up?

Was there an established etiquette for dates that didn't happen?

How would it affect my time at the halfway house?

Maybe I shouldn't have agreed to this with someone I saw on a regular basis. If things went poorly, there would be no getting away from my failure.

It wasn't too late to call it off. I had Kenneth's number. I could call him right now and tell him I wasn't able to make it.

"Clay?"

Too late.

I turned to greet Kenneth with a smile.

"Hey. There you are. I didn't see you arrive in this rain."

He was a little wet but had managed to avoid getting too soaked by darting immediately under the theater awning like I had. His short dark bangs were stuck to his forehead with water, and he ran his fingers through them to try and put his hair back into place.

"I was hoping the weather would hold out a little longer, but I'm never that lucky." There wasn't much he could do while his hair was still wet, so he gave up after a moment with a nervous chuckle. "I'm glad you're here. I was half convinced that you weren't going to show up or would bail on me last minute."

"What? No, we agreed to meet, so of course I'm going to show," I lied, keeping the fact that I'd nearly done exactly as he feared firmly locked behind my teeth.

The rushing sound of the rain made it hard to talk, so we stepped inside the movie kiosk to take shelter behind the safety of closed doors.

As we both silently considered the movies currently playing, I couldn't help looking around at the other people present. More than half of them were couples. It was easy to tell from the way they stood next to each other, often with their arms around each other. Even the ones who weren't blatantly holding onto each other at least stood close enough to touch in some way.

I eyed the space between Kenneth and myself. Like this, we looked no different than friends.

Other than physical intimacy, what was the difference between a date and just hanging out with a friend?

Nothing really. Take sex out of the equation, and I saw no difference between romance and friendship.

I already knew how to handle friendship, so maybe this wouldn't be so bad.

One of the movies on the list caught my eye and I pointed it out. It was an adaptation of a book I'd recently read. I'd liked the book and was curious to see if the movie would be equally as enjoyable.

"What? That?" Kenneth said when I pointed it out. "It's a kid's movie. It'll be boring."

Oh, right.

The books I read were all middle school or high school books. That meant the movies made from them would be targeted toward the same audience. I'd grown so used to my reading choices being treated as normal, that I'd forgotten that most adults aren't interested in "kid stuff".

I was about to argue that we could still enjoy the movie even if it was meant for a young audience, when I noticed Kenneth searching though his wallet. He was counting the bills inside, trying not to draw attention to himself as he grimaced over the number.

I didn't know what Kenneth's financial situation was, but the fact that he was living in a halfway house meant it probably wasn't good. I had a job, and a brother who supported me. While I wasn't rich, I wasn't struggling anymore either.

Between the two of us, it was more important for him to enjoy the movie because it was going to cost him more.

"You're right," I said, plastering a smile on my face that I hoped seemed genuine. "I haven't actually watched many movies, so I don't know what's out right now. Why don't you pick one out for us."

"Really?" Kenneth flashed me a genuine smile. "Thanks!"

We ended up buying tickets for some random action movie I'd never heard of. As we headed for the theater, we passed the snack stand without a word, both of us pretending it didn't exist.

Candy and snacks were a luxury I loved to indulge in, much to the grievance of my waistline, but the prices I could see listed behind the snack stand were criminal. I may not be hurting for money, but even I couldn't justify such an expense.

Half the theater was filled by the time we got there, so we found a pair of seats near the back wall, as far from others as possible. As we waited for the movie to start, Kenneth and I talked for a bit, sticking to general topics such as games we'd played, books we'd read, and so on.

It didn't take long for me to come to the realization that we had almost nothing in common.

Literally, after fifteen minutes of trying and failing to find common ground, it seemed like being gay was our only shared interest.

Luckily, the movie started before things could get too awkward and we had an excuse to stop talking.

I was bored.

Only twenty minutes in, and the hero had already escaped three different gun fights through increasingly absurd means. I was fighting the urge to close my eyes and fall asleep, but at least in the seat next to me Kenneth seemed to be enjoying himself.

At the halfway point of the movie, I'd stopped paying attention and had no idea what was going on. I made up a game in my head, imagining outlandish things that could happen in the movie. I'd just drawn up a scenario where aliens suddenly descended and abducted all the characters, when I felt an unexpected touch against my hand.

I pulled away instinctively, and a spike of fear gripped my heart. Glancing over, terrified of what I would see, I found Kenneth slowly withdrawing his hand and placing it back on the armrest.

I felt bad. It seemed like he'd merely been trying to hold my hand. That was something that people who were dating did but letting him touch me wasn't the same as letting him pick the movie. The feeling of hands grabbing me in the dark was too familiar and brought back more memories than I was prepared to deal with. That was one concession I couldn't give him.

I sat with both my hands tucked safely in my lap for the rest of the movie.

Afterward, as we stood outside the theater under the awning, waiting for our respective Ubers to arrive, Kenneth tried reaching for my hand again, but didn't look shocked when I pulled away.

He sighed, but the sound was mostly swallowed by the rain.

"You aren't really interested in dating me, are you?"

I opened my mouth to argue, but no words came out.

What could I say?

I refused to lie to him. He didn't deserve that, but I also couldn't think of anything to say that wouldn't sound insulting.

All I could give him was the truth, even if it was uncomfortable or confusing.

"Honestly, I don't know what I want." I ran a hand through my hair and grimaced when my fingers snagged on several knots. My wavy hair had always tangled easily, especially in wet weather.

I didn't try to pull through the knots

and just left them in place to be brushed out properly later.

Kenneth scowled down at his feet, not even looking at me as he buried both hands in his pockets.

"I probably shouldn't have gotten my hopes up. You're way to pretty for me."

I hated it when people complimented my physical appearance. It was too close to the compliments that clients would often say to me when they thought it would get them a better deal. Or worse, the way my captors would admire me like they were praising themselves for their own good taste.

Instead of getting upset though, I kept my expression neutral as I sought a way to explain myself.

"It's not like that. You did nothing wrong. This is on me. I don't know what I want. I don't even know if I'm ready to start dating, but I figured the only way to figure it out would be to try. I'm sorry if that's disappointing."

I expected him to be mad, or maybe even hurt.

What I didn't expect was for him to start laughing.

"Are you really trying the *'its not you,*

it's me', line?"

"Um... Yes? Is that a bad thing?"

I'd never heard that line before, but Kenneth's reaction said that it was well known. There was a lot of supposedly common knowledge I was lacking, and it had gotten me into trouble before. Maybe that line "it's not you it's me," had a negative meaning that I didn't know about.

Kenneth stared at me in shock. "You really don't recognize..." He trailed off, but his gaze flickered down to my hands, which I kept tucked firmly close to me.

Something seemed to occur to him, though I couldn't tell what.

"You're not ready," he eventually concluded. "I get it. I really do. We've all been through some shit. I hope, when you are ready, you'll know what you're looking for."

Most dates ended with a kiss, or maybe a hug.

Ours ended with a handshake.

It was an extremely awkward experience, but as I climbed into the back of my Uber driver's car, I found that I was glad for the experience anyway.

I'd tried. That had to count for

something.

After giving the driver Jason's address, I pulled out my phone intending to call Logan.

Over the last year, I usually talked to him about once a week, and it had become a habit for me to call him after something noteworthy happened in my life. I looked forward to hearing his praise when I succeeded, or listening to his insightful analysis when I was confused.

My finger hovered over the call button. I'd never hesitated to call him before, but when I imagined telling him about my attempt at dating, my stomach turned several uncomfortable flips. I didn't want him to know what I'd done tonight. I felt like I'd done something wrong, and even the thought of talking to Logan about dating filled me with tangle of unpleasant emotions.

I shoved my phone back in my pocket.

There was no reason to tell Logan about my date right away. I could tell him later.

For now, I would keep it to myself.

CHAPTER TWENTY

Logan

MY KNEES HURT from crouching behind the couch for so long. While I shouldn't be surprised about the lack of punctuality among criminals, I still wished they would show up when they were supposed to.

Thanks to Clay and Jordy's information, we'd made great strides in the Bell ringer case. The Federal Protection Agency, a special task force focusing on crimes against children, had originally been formed out of members of law enforcement from several different states, as well as a few members of the FBI. Several private investigation firms, such as Alias Investigations had even been brought in shortly after the FPA's inception. Recently, our numbers had grown again and there were many new faces in the FPA offices, and that meant more people working on this case, too.

Not only were the streets of Baton Rouge being cleaned up, but many other places as well.

In any other case, that kind of collaboration would have been cause for celebration, but our enemies were such a large, deeply rooted organization that even with so such manpower and resources, we were still struggling to make headway.

Recently, we'd managed to crack their access to one home security system. There was more, but even taking out one point of access would be a step in the right direction.

At least, that had been the original plan until my friend Roland, of all people, came up with a better idea.

Instead of shutting them out, we should use their own backdoor into the home security system to secretly monitor them and try to catch them in the act.

It had taken nearly a year to get to this

point, but all that effort led me to my current position, kneeling behind the couch in a stranger's home, waiting for our target to come through the door. The family that lived here was currently barricaded upstairs to keep them out of harm's way. We'd only been able to loop the camera's signal long enough to sneak a few agents, such as myself, into the house, and couldn't risk evacuating the family in case our target noticed.

Luckily, the family had been willing to cooperate, though they were obviously terrified.

That had been hours ago. It was now nearing two in the morning. Based on the family's usual routine, this would be the perfect time to sneak in.

So where were the fuckers?

As the minutes ticked by, and worry churned over and over in my brain, the soft crackle of my comm interrupted my thoughts.

"Be advised. Suspicious activity spotted on the north side of the house."

I knew the same information echoed through the comms of the two other agents carefully stationed in the house, and it would also be heard by many others hidden throughout the neighborhood.

Another agent, Gloria Stayner, who I'd only just met a few days ago and had been assigned as the leader of our infiltration team, responded back.

"Can you be more specific? It'd be nice how many people are coming."

"Negative," the voice on the earpiece responded. "Visual confirmation was minimal. Assuming this is our target, they are being careful to stay out of sight."

The team leader sighed audibly. "They've had a lot longer to study the area than we have. They probably have every streetlight, porch light, and security system in the entire neighborhood memorized. Everyone, stay alert and be ready for anything."

Two minutes later, the telltale sound of the front door lock clicking open could be heard through the otherwise empty house.

From her position behind an armchair near the door, the team leader held up a fist in a silent signal to hold our positions.

I waited with my hand on my gun, but still kept the weapon holstered. Cold sweat dripped down the sides of my temples as I stared into the dark, my gaze fixed on the door.

The door opened. At least three people slipped inside. It was so dark I couldn't see any details, but based on the shape of the shadows, I was almost certain it was only three people.

We could take three people. Hell, I'd take all three down myself if I had to.

The three intruders closed the door behind them and navigated through the house with the ease of people who had already memorized the layout.

Still, Agent Stayner signaled for us to stay where we were.

Logically, I knew why. The targets were still too close to the front door. If we revealed ourselves now, they might be able to get away.

Still, it was nearly impossible to wait while the target of my fury was right in front of me.

It would have been easier to hold back a volcano with only my bare hands, I bit the inside of my cheek until I tasted blood in order to keep myself hidden behind that couch.

The intruders were nearly to the stairs leading to the upper floor when our team leader finally gave us the signal to move. She turned on the light in the dining room, which was far enough away to illuminate the area without blinding us, and I jumped up from behind the couch.

My gaze locked onto the nearest target, focusing solely on the gun in their hand. I never even looked at their face, as I disarmed their weapon and slipped around behind them to lock my arms around their neck in a chokehold. Their nails scratched desperately at my arm, but the long thick sleeves of my shirt protected me and made their struggles useless. Without any blood flowing to their brain, it took only thirty seconds for them to grow weak, and I lowered their body to the ground without releasing my hold on them.

Soon enough, they lost consciousness, but I still didn't let go.

"Hollingsworth," the Gloria shouted from across the room. "Hollingsworth. The bastard's already unconscious. Let go before you kill him. We need to bring them all in alive."

Growling low under my breath, I was so tempted to ignore the order and keep squeezing until the body under me stopped breathing. This monster harmed kids in the worst way possible. For all I knew, it could be one of the very people responsible for what had happened to Clay.

It was the thought of Clay that managed to calm me down and convince me to let go. In the year since I'd taken him to Maryland, he was doing so much better, and working his way toward healing. He needed justice the proper way. Vigilante murder wouldn't help him, and it would probably get me booted from the case.

Standing up, I looked over at the team leader, where she had a struggling man pinned face down on the floor in a very efficient and painful armlock. She nodded at me, before returning her focus to her own target. My moment of almost-insubordination seemed to have been forgiven.

While I'd decided not to kill the man I'd taken down, I couldn't help using my foot to kick his unconscious body over onto its back with more force than necessary.

I don't know what I was expecting to see, but whatever my expectations were, they were significantly underwhelmed. In my mind, these Bell ringers were tantamount to monsters straight out of a child's fable. The kind that parents would use to warm their children away from wandering off into the woods alone.

Yet, the person on the floor before me was just a guy. Not particularly old or young, and there was nothing outstanding about his appearance. It was the kind of man I wouldn't have looked twice at if I passed him on the street.

Was it better or worse that the monster hunting kids in the dark was just a human?

Sudden shouting made me jump and raise my gun. Near the staircase, the third target had managed to slip away from the agent trying to subdue him, and stood with his back to the wall, gun in hand.

"Get away from me. I've done nothing wrong."

The absurdity of the statement made me snort under my breath. I would never understand the inner workings of these people's minds, but surely this man couldn't be delusional enough to think himself innocent.

The agent that had accidentally let their target go was obviously peeved about the mistake and pointed their own weapon at the man with a calm hand and a steady gaze.

"So, breaking into other people's homes is just a harmless hobby is it," they taunted the man. "Give it up. This is the end of the line for you. Come quietly and you won't get hurt."

"No," the man shouted as his gaze darted from side to side, looking for any possible escape. "I've been to prison once. I'm not going back."

He raised his gun with intent, and for a moment, I feared he was about to commit suicide-by-cop and force us to shoot him. However, his gun never pointed at any of us, and instead he kept raising it until the barrel pressed against his own temple.

"No," our team leader shouted, but it was too late.

The man pulled the trigger, and the wall beside him was painted red.

I stared at the freshly dead body that dropped to the floor and tried to summon an ounce of sympathy. Death should be sad, and a loss of life should never be taken lightly.

Yet, I felt nothing but a vague sense of

relief, like finding out that the dirty dishes in the sink had already been washed and I could cross that chore off my list.

Maybe I needed to go back to therapy for a bit. This case seemed to be affecting me more than I realized if that was my only reaction to watching someone commit suicide in front of me.

With one target dead and one unconscious, arresting them didn't take very long. The one conscious target complied silently with every instruction we gave him and didn't utter a word as we shoved him into the back of a cop car in handcuffs beside his unconscious accomplice.

The dead body would be taken to the morgue and dealt with accordingly. Even criminals had a family, and they had a right to bury their loved one. If a member of my family turned out to be involved in something like the Bell ringers, I'd have them cremated and dump their ashes in a distant landfill, but I kept that suggestion to myself.

We had just set the two living targets off in a cop car, when new information came through the radios. An unlicensed van had been caught trying to flee the area. It had been stopped, but the agents were now in a standoff as the driver refused to exit the vehicle.

With a quick order, Agent Stayner directed us to the site of the standoff.

Just like the man I'd taken down, the van was also completely unremarkable. It looked more like the kind of oversized minivan a mother would use to take a horde of kids to soccer practice, rather than a tool for kidnapping. The only thing suspicious about it was how fast it had been driving away from the scene of the crime, and the fact that its license plate had a quick release catch that would allow it to be swapped out at a moment's notice.

It was only through sheer luck that I arrived just in time to hear the request for permission to shoot the target in the van.

"Wait," I jumped forward to interject. "Don't do that."

Our team leader was the highest-ranking officer present and had taken over command of the situation as soon as she arrived. She looked at me with a question in her eyes as she held the radio up ready to reply to the request.

"We've already apprehended two

suspects alive. Keeping this one alive isn't vital to the mission and extracting him from the car alive will put our agents in a lot more risk."

"I know, but..." I gestured toward the van. "Look at the size of the vehicle. The targeted family only had one prospective victim, and a single child doesn't take up much space. There's no reason for them to have a van this large. even if it was meant to transport all four members of their team, it's still bigger than they would need."

Agent Stayner's eyes narrowed under the glare of the streetlight as she studied the van. "You think there might be others?"

"Other kids. Other perpetrators. I don't know, but something about it doesn't sit right with me. We can't open fire when we don't know for certain what we're firing at."

Thankfully, the team leader listened to me and denied the order to open fire.

"All right, Hollingsworth. Got any more bright ideas about how to get the target out of the van without gunfire."

I glanced toward the van again, making sure it was designed the way I thought it was. Although it resembled a minivan, it still had large double doors at the back like a cargo van.

"We pretend like we're going to use deadly force to keep the target occupied. Meanwhile, someone sneaks around back and opens the back door. We can sneak up on the target, hopefully, or at least get a better look at what's waiting for us inside."

"All right." The team leader relayed these instructions through the radio, before giving me a smirk. "You know how to pick a lock, Hollingsworth?"

I nodded hesitantly, already suspecting where this was going.

"Then, since this is your idea, you get the honor of doing the sneaking."

I sighed, but I wasn't unhappy about the outcome. I probably would have volunteered anyway, but there was something annoying about being ordered to do it when the plan had been mine from the start.

There wasn't any time to waste. Within a minute, I managed to sneak around through a few back yards to put myself behind the van without the target seeing me. As soon as I was in place, several heavily armed agents approached the van from the front, making a big scene and shouting threats at the target to keep his attention pointed forward.

My lock picking skills were rustier than I'd like, and took me more than one attempt, but I managed to get the back of the van unlocked and cracked the door open just enough to peek inside.

Some of the seats had been pulled out of the van to create empty space at the back. A rough brown blanket covered something that at first seemed like supplies, until I noticed the blanket moving. There were people under the blanket, and based on the size, they weren't adults.

The only adult in the van that I could see was the driver. From this angle, I would have a perfect shot at the back of his head. He'd never even know I was here before he died.

Vengeance would be sweet, but that wasn't why I was here. I needed to get the kids out and let the other agents handle the driver.

I opened the door as little as possible and kept myself low so the van's seats would cover me as I grabbed the kids, blanket and all. The two bodies I felt were much smaller than I expected and took almost no effort to pick them up.

The driver shouted when he noticed what I was doing, but I pulled the kids out of the van and kicked the door shut before he could even turn around.

As I ran down the street with a small body in each arm, I heard the chaos of open gunfire rattle the air behind me.

Once a safe distance away from the violence, I set my burdens down on the side of the curb and pulled the blankets away.

A pair of children blinked up at me with terrified eyes. A boy and a girl, both under the age of ten. They were bound and gagged, with heavy tear tracks down their cheeks, and both looked to be on the verge of hyperventilating.

"It's okay," I said with the same soothing tone I'd used with Clay when I approached him in his apartment. "I'm not going to hurt you. You're safe. Okay? Just let me get these off you."

With careful fingers, I reached for the gag in the girl's mouth, but she pulled back and shook her head.

"No, wait. It's okay. It's okay." I tried to

explain, but it didn't work. To them I was just another adult that wanted to hurt them.

"Here. Look."

I pulled out my badge and held it up for them to see. They stopped struggling but didn't seem any more inclined to let me near them.

"See this badge? I'm like a cop. The police. That means I protect people. Understand?"

The kids' eyes remained narrowed in suspicion, but this time they didn't pull away when I reached for them, and I was able to remove their restraints.

As soon as they were free and they realized I wasn't trying to trick them, both kids immediately started crying and dove back into my arms. I held them right there on the side of the street, whispering words of comfort as we waited for the rest of the situation to calm down.

There was one other thing I'd noticed, though. Neither of these kids was blond.

The daughter of the family that we'd protected earlier perfectly fit the description of the Bell ringer's usual targets. She could have been a female version of Clay when he was younger.

These two, however, were completely different. Based on their ages, they were a better fit for the preferred victims of the pedophile ring that Alias Investigations had brought down.

It was just more evidence for what we already suspected. These two trafficking rings, which had originally seemed like independent cases, were just branches of a much larger tree. There was no telling how many branches this tree had, but tonight proved that they were not only organized, but also helping each other.

While I was glad we saved these victims tonight, it also brought a sense of despair.

No matter how many branches we cut off, this criminal tree would never die until its roots were dug up.

I wasn't sure if we had a shovel large enough for the task.

CHAPTER TWENTY-ONE

Logan

TWO DAYS LATER, I woke up in my bed, gasping for air, and with the phantom taste of Clay lingering on my lips. I'd been hoping that my dreams about Clay would eventually fade away as the distance between us remained, but it was going on a year now since I'd parted from him, and the dreams only seemed to be getting more frequent. They'd be driving me insane if I didn't enjoy them so much. I'd considered cutting contact with him to solve the problem—out of sight out of mind, as the saying goes—but I couldn't bear to do such a thing. Not only did I look forward to his video calls, but I knew suddenly disappearing would also hurt him. I wouldn't be able to explain why I needed to cut contact. To Clay, it would seem like I suddenly ghosted him for no reason.

No. I couldn't do that to him. He'd been hurt and abandoned by enough people in his life. I didn't need to add myself to that list.

So, I dutifully maintained our weekly video calls and tried to ignore the effects of my dreams as much as possible.

I glanced at the clock. It wasn't time for me to get up yet, but there also wasn't enough time for me to go back to sleep. In the end, I decided to just start my day early. Arriving at the office before my shift started wasn't going to do any harm, and maybe I could get a head start on the endless paperwork that waited for me.

The FPA office was never empty, but so early in the morning, there weren't many people either. After dropping my stuff off at my desk, I noticed the light on in Mason's office. Mason Wright was always the first to arrive and the last to leave every day. I had no idea how he managed to find time for a life outside his job, but every rumor about him said that he was also a dutiful family man.

Since he was also Roland's brother, I could personally attest that these rumors about our leader were accurate.

With so few people in the office, it would be a good time to give Mason an account of our recent mission. It had been a day and a half since we rescued several kids from being kidnapped and brought four members of the Bell ringers to justice, one way or another. By now, Mason must have already received the details about everything that happened from Agent Stayner, but I knew he would also want to hear a firsthand account directly from me. So, I knocked on his door then poked my head inside.

He was on the phone and pointed over to the corner of his office in a silent order for me to wait. I stepped aside and closed the door behind me, ready to wait as long as necessary. Any call Mason took on the office phone had to be important, because he only gave that number out for official business.

I occupied myself counting the cracks in the ceiling, until Mason's conversation caught my attention.

Maryland?

Why was he talking about Maryland?

Listening in, I couldn't tell what the conversation was about, but it seemed to include a list of different places all over the country.

Nearly ten minutes later, I was bursting with curiosity when he finally hung up the phone.

"Logan. I assume this is about your recent mission. I've got the report right here. So, how'd it go? Seems like it was even more successful than we expected."

"Oh, uh, yeah." The conversation I overheard had completely derailed my thoughts process, and I struggled to remember why I'd even stepped into the office.

I gave Mason a basic summary of what had happened the other night, but I barely paid attention to what I was saying.

One word resonated over and over in my mind.

Maryland.

When I finished, Mason thanked me and casually dismissed me from his office, but I hung near the door, debating with myself.

"Um, Mason," I said before I'd fully decided to open my mouth. "What was that call about earlier? It seemed... important."

I expected to be ignored, or maybe outright scolded for being nosy, but instead Mason just sighed and ran an exasperated hand through his hair before staring forlornly at his phone.

"We've been making a lot of progress with this Bell ringer case."

"Okay? And that's a good thing, so what's the problem?"

He sighed again, and for the first time, I noticed slivers of gray at his temples. He wasn't old, but he was no longer a young man either. Being the leader of the FPA was difficult under normal conditions, but with the extra workload we'd had recently, he was obviously feeling the strain.

"Success is good, yes. But the aftermath often leaves us with a lot of victims that need to be taken care of. Even this most recent mission brought us two extra victims we weren't expecting."

The image of the two children I'd pulled out of the van flashed before my eyes, and I could still feel their weight in my arms.

"Yes, we're saving people. Kids. That's our job."

I still wasn't seeing the problem. Mason was talking about our success as if it was a bad thing.

Did he want us to not save people?

"Our job is about more than just protecting them for a single moment. It's in the job description. Protect and serve. Protecting is easy, but serving is a lot more difficult. Many of these victims don't have families that can take care of them. We have to find some place for them, but resources are limited. Most care homes and foster facilities aren't equipped for the type of severe trauma that the victims we rescue are suffering from, and the facilities that can handle it are already filled to capacity. To put it simply, we're running out of safe places to put the victims we rescue."

His earlier conversation that I'd overheard finally made more sense, though I was still confused about the location.

"So, you're reaching out to other facilities for help to find placement for the victims. But why go so far as Maryland?"

Mason's desk was always

immaculately clean. He never took out more than one thing at a time, and always put it back before moving on to something else. When he pulled out, not one, but three different folders and spread them over his desk simultaneously, I knew he was stressed.

"We aren't the only ones facing this problem. The recent combined efforts on the Bell ringer case have caused a similar over-taxation of resources in many areas. We're having to look farther and farther away to find accommodation for victims. Those kids you saved the other day need to be placed somewhere, and a facility in Maryland is the closest place I've found with vacancies."

Gritting his teeth and growling low under his breath, he slammed one of the files closed, nearly knocking it right off the desk.

"At least, that's the plan. Getting them to Maryland is proving to be nearly impossible. There's no budget for three last minute plane tickets since their caseworker has to go with them. A long car trip will be stressful for them, but it's looking like the only option."

This wasn't part of my job. Finding

safe placement for victims was someone else's responsibility. I should have just turned around and walked out of the office door.

But I didn't, and I wasn't even surprised with myself.

"I can fly them to Maryland."

"Huh?" Mason looked at me with a confused expression.

"I can fly them to Maryland. The kids and the caseworker. I'm still licensed to fly since I served in the Air Force. Plus, I've got some old buddies from my time serving that still owe me a favor. I can probably convince them to lend me the use of a plane." I approached the desk with my hands held out in a beseeching gesture, practically begging Mason to agree with me.

"It'll be easier for everyone this way. The caseworker won't be overwhelmed taking care of two kids alone, and the kids already know me since I was the one who rescued them. We can have them relocated in just a couple of hours."

Mason ran his hands through his hair again. If he kept it up, he was going to go bald as well as gray.

"This is more than I should be asking

of you, but I also can't afford to turn you down. All right. I'll redirect any new cases to give you some time free and see if I can scrape any funds together, so you don't have to pay for everything out of pocket."

It took another hour to plan out all the details, and when I left Mason's office, I was scheduled to get on a plane the very next day.

By then, more people had arrived at the office. I turned and headed straight for the door that led to the building's rooftop staircase. Along the way I nodded to people, and exchanged friendly greetings, but if asked later, I couldn't have said who I encountered. My body was on autopilot, and my brain was a dizzying whirlwind of thoughts that kept flying around but refused to land long enough for me to focus on them.

On the roof, a strong wind whipped at my hair and made my eyes water as I looked out over the city. In the distance, I could just see the Mississippi River and the twin peaks of the Horace Wilkinson Bridge that stretched across it. The bridge was usually a dull iron gray, but in the morning sunlight it seemed to glow as if made from pure copper.

My phone sat cold and lifeless in my hand. At first, I'd thought to call Clay and tell him I was going to be making a trip to Maryland, but I changed my mind before hitting a single button.

Mason was fooled, and so was everyone else, but I couldn't fool myself. Volunteering to make the trip to Maryland wasn't a selfless act for the sake of helping victims. I'd barely even thought about those kids when I made the suggestion.

No.

Only one thought had been in my mind.

If I went to Maryland, there was a chance I might see Clay again.

It was selfish. He was building a life of his own. He didn't need me to show up out of the blue. Especially after the dreams I'd been having about him. Even if I kept the nature of my dreams a secret and never told a soul, they would still be in the back of my mind when I saw him again.

Would I be able to keep my cool and pretend like nothing had changed?

That I wasn't constantly thinking about him in ways that he hadn't consented to?

Maybe.

If I was any sort of decent person I would go back into Mason's office and offer to find someone else to make the flight to Maryland. I would keep myself far away from Clay and only talk to him through the safety of a video call and many miles between us.

But I wouldn't. At this point, I couldn't. The idea of going to Maryland was like a siren's call, luring me from the safety of my home and tow myself upon the dangerous rocks of a distant shore.

I wouldn't make any plans, or even tell Clay I was coming, but somehow, I knew I'd end up meeting him anyway. That was how fate always worked, placing you in the path of the one thing you should stay away from.

I should be disgusted with myself, but all I felt was excited at the prospect of finally laying my eyes on him again.

CHAPTER TWENTY-TWO

Clay

DOMINIC'S PLACE WAS getting new guests. This wasn't strange, people were always coming and going from the halfway house, but the new arrivals were apparently younger than usual. Dominic was one of the few halfway houses that employed full-time staff as well as volunteers, and he even had a few employees that were specially trained to care for young kids. This was exactly why he was expanding his facility into an apartment complex as well, so he could better separate the younger kids from the older adults, and so everyone could get more specialized care, but until the expansion was complete, he needed all the help he could get.

The actual staff were busy getting ready for the new arrivals and planning how to care for them, so I'd volunteered to get the room ready.

It wasn't much. The room already had a bunkbed, a double closet, and a pair of matching desks. I just needed to check everything to make sure it was clean and dust free, and make up the beds with sheets and pillows so they were ready for use. The process only took me about an hour.

Just as I was fluffing the last pillow into place, Leslie poked her head through the doorway.

"The new arrivals are here. They're downstairs talking to Dominic now."

I smoothed out the sheets one last time, then followed her downstairs.

Before I even reached the bottom of the stairs, I could already hear Dominic's laughter. He had a natural affinity with children and was no doubt already making them feel right at home.

Just as I suspected, when I reached the bottom of the stairs, the first thing I saw was Dominic kneeling on the floor with a boy and a girl, playing with them and making them laugh right along with him. The kids' social service worker was standing beside them, calmly explaining something I couldn't hear over the sound of the kid's joy. Whatever she was saying must have been serious, because there was a frown on her face, but she didn't seem angry. Just very focused.

Then I noticed someone else standing behind the social service worker, and my heart stopped.

"Logan!"

My shouting caused everyone in the room to jump in surprise, but I didn't care as I raced down the last few steps and threw myself at the man I hadn't seen in person for a year. I wrapped my arms around him and barely resisted the urge to wrap my legs around him too and cling like a baby koala to a tree.

Logan was a few inches taller than me, so when he held me, my feet didn't quite touch the ground. His arms didn't even tremble as they supported my weight.

"Clay?"

His greeting was surprisingly uncertain, and I pulled back just enough to see the bewildered look on his face.

"What? What's wrong?"

"Nothing, I just..." He looked around the room like he was only just seeing it for the first time. "I wasn't expecting to see you."

"Oh." I released my grip from around him enough for my feet to slide back to the floor. The excitement I'd felt over his sudden appearance fizzled but didn't completely fade.

There were at least a dozen people in the front room of the facility, and every single one of them was watching us with curiosity. Even the two new kids stared at me with their big eyes.

Embarrassed, I tried to back away, but Logan's grip on my shoulders didn't let me retreat more than a single step.

"What, um... what are you doing here?"

Logan nodded toward the kids that were still huddled near Dominic. "These two needed a ride from Louisiana to Maryland, so I volunteered my services."

"You drove them here?" I eyed the kids again and swallowed hard around the ball of jealousy that swelled up in my throat. I was the one that Logan had driven across the country to save. Now, these two little kids had replaced me.

Logan had a job to do. He was moving on to helping other victims. I should be happy about that, but it just made me feel bitter.

"Actually, I flew them here," Logan said, completely oblivious to the spiteful thoughts stabbing inside my brain at that very moment. "Faster than a car ride, and cheaper than buying plane tickets last minute."

"Oh, you can fly a plane?" I tried to sound upbeat and invested in the conversation, but my words felt wrong on my tongue, and I was certain my tone sounded off.

"Yeah. I told you about my time in the Air Force. I'm still licensed to fly, and an old service buddy loaned me his plane."

Looking around the room, he finally noticed everyone staring at us. "Hey. I think we're causing a distraction. Why don't you show me around the place, and we'll let everyone else get the kids settled in."

Dominic's place didn't look that big from the outside, but it was deceptive. The building went a lot further back than it seemed from the front. It was not only a halfway house, but was also a pseudo-orphanage for young kids with nowhere else to go.

I showed Logan around, focusing on the facilities that the kids he'd brought would probably need. There was in-house therapy, an on-call doctor, and even tutors who came in regularly. I'd used the tutors myself to help get my education back on track, so I could attest to their quality.

In turn, Logan told me about his most recent mission. He couldn't disclose all the details, but it was enough for me to get an idea of what had happened.

He was still fighting to bring down the trafficking ring that had kidnapped me, which was turning out to be a lot bigger and more powerful than I'd originally known. He'd not only caught a group of kidnappers in the act, but also pulled those two kids out of the back of a van and saved them from being spirited away.

My teeth ground together so hard my jaw ached.

Why were they lucky enough to be saved when I wasn't?

Where had all this effort been when I

was taken?

My brother had been forced to use his own time and money to hire private investigators to look for me, and I was only found after my captors had already let me go.

A monstrosity of a playground stood at the very center of the building, surrounded with walls like a courtyard. It had been built to look like a massive tree, with the playground built in like a tree house.

Logan guided me over to the swings that hung from one of the branches, convincing me to sit in one of the plastic seats before claiming the other for himself.

The structure was made for kids, so our knees came up ridiculously high when our feet were planted on the ground. Logan stretched his legs out over the ground and crossed his ankles as he swayed back and forth on the swing.

"Hey, Clay? Are you really all right? You seem… more subdued than usual."

Rather than copy his posture, I stood on the seat of the swing and gripped the chains in both hands to keep my balance.

"To be honest, I'm jealous."

Standing on the seat while he was sitting had the advantage of putting my head far above his, so I didn't have to look directly into his eyes. It almost gave me the courage to admit everything I'd been feeling.

Almost.

The words were right on the tip of my tongue, but at the last second, I chickened out and swallowed them again.

Instead, I tapped his shoulder with my foot and adopted a joking tone.

"I've never ridden in an airplane before. If you've got access to a plane, how come you've never offered to take me for a flight?"

"Okay."

His easy answer nearly knocked me off the swing, and chains rattled as I clung to them to stay upright.

"What?"

Without even looking, I knew Logan was smiling up at me.

"I've got to fly the social worker back when she's done here, but it's going to take several days to get the kids settled into their new place, so I'm stuck here for the time being. If you want to go for a flight, then sure, I can take you. Just say when.”

Climbing down from the swing, I sat on the seat properly instead, so this time my eye line was equal with his.

“When.” My joke went over his head and he looked at me with the confusion of a puppy dog that didn’t understand why its treat had disappeared. “You said ‘say when’. So... when.”

It was a lame joke, but once Logan understood what I meant, he laughed anyway.

“You want to go right now? Sure. Just let me get checked into my hotel and I’ll come back to pick you up in about an hour.”

When we left the playground, the hallways were suspiciously absent of people. I suspected that everyone else was keeping out of our way to give us space. I would have been embarrassed, but I was too grateful for the illusion of privacy.

At the front door, just before he left, Logan turned back to me and grabbed my hand. “Since you were honest with me, I should be honest as well. I lied to you earlier.”

My hand clenched tight around his.

He’d lied?

Was he not happy to see me, or had he changed his mind about taking me on his plane?

Still holding onto my hand, his other hand rubbed nervously at the back of his head. "I didn't *know* for certain that you were going to be here, but I also wasn't surprised. I just had a feeling that if I made this trip, I'd run into you. It was part of the reason I volunteered. I hope that's not weird." Pink colored his cheeks at the admission.

My heartbeat was still in my ears when I bumped our shoulders together.

"It's not weird. I'm glad you wanted to see me." I flashed him a smile.

With his confession out in the open, Logan seemed much happier, and walked away from the building with smile on his lips and a bounce in his step.

I watched him leave, wishing I could feel as carefree as he looked, but my own thoughts still weighed heavily on me.

He'd said I was honest with him, but that was a lie. I hadn't been honest at all. If I were truly honest, I would have told him the real reason for my jealousy. I didn't care about the plane ride. I just wanted his care and attention all to myself.

Logan wasn't the only one I was lying to. I'd been lying to myself for a year now. Every time he called me, and we spent hours just discussing our day, every time I felt a thrill just from hearing his name, I lied to myself about my feelings for him. I insisted that what I felt was friendship, and anything else was just gratitude from the way he helped me.

Ever since my disastrous date with Kenneth that lie had slowly been eroding.

I couldn't keep lying to myself. What I felt for Logan was beyond friendship. I was in love with him, and worse, I was attracted to him.

The thought nearly made me laugh out loud.

Who would want someone like me lusting after them?

My desires had no value. If anything, I'd just end up tainting him.

He'd surely leave and never come back if he knew the way I thought about him sometimes, and how the feeling of his arms around me made me feel.

I would just have to keep these thoughts to myself. Our friendship was too important to be spoiled by my impure thoughts.

My hand felt cold despite the summer heat. I was already missing his touch after only a few minutes apart.

This was going to be a very difficult vow to keep.

CHAPTER TWENTY-THREE

Clay

MY STOMACH SWOOPED with a feeling of weightlessness before we even stepped foot in the plane. It was a small thing with only a few seats. The only planes I'd ever seen were commercial sized ones that carried hundreds of people, so this small contraption didn't seem at all sturdy enough to get us airborne.

Under any other circumstances, I would have been terrified as I sat down in the cockpit seat within arm's reach of the dizzying number of controls. Yet, as Logan sat in the seat next to me and his arm brushed mine, all I could focus on was his scent.

He was clean like soap and fresh air, with a bright note to his scent that made me think of sunlight filtering through green leaves. I'd forgotten what he smelled like. It was such a silly thing to worry about, but the fact that I could forget any part of him left me terrified.

If I could forget this, what else could I forget about him?

His voice.

His smile.

The color of his eyes.

If enough time passed, could I forget him completely?

With an impressive amount of confidence, Logan went through the sequence of starting up the plane and getting ready for takeoff. I never realized how much communication it required from other people, but he had to get confirmation from at least three different voices through the plane's radio before we could even leave the hangar where the small plane was parked.

I clung to the arms of the chair with a death grip as we started moving. The runway area was completely flat, which created an optical illusion as if we were barely going anywhere, but I could feel the momentum of the plane around us and knew the tarmac was passing by just feet below us.

Beside me, Logan laughed and placed a comforting hand over mine on the arm of my chair.

"It's okay. Take a deep breath. I've done this a million times. We'll be fine."

"Tell me that when we're in the air," I snapped at him though gritted teeth. "And keep your eyes on the road. Or the air. Or whatever you need to watch."

Logan laughed again but didn't say anything as he obeyed my order and focused on what he was doing. The plane crept across the tarmac, passing several other much larger aircraft that looked like they could run us over without even noticing. Apparently, even airplanes had to obey the laws of the queue and we waited for our turn at the start of the runway.

I got to watch several planes take off from an up-close view, and each time I still marveled at the fact that they were able to fly. It didn't seem like it should work. These clunky metal beasts had neither the agility of birds, nor the delicacy of bugs, yet as soon as they got going fast enough their noses turned toward the sky and they left the ground behind.

Eventually, it was our turn and I clung to my chair so hard my fingertips turned white.

"Tell me when it's over," I said, though I never closed my eyes.

"We don't have to do this," Logan assured me, even as he was given final clearance for takeoff. "We can turn around right now and go back to the hangar."

"No. I want to. I'm just... nervous."

I was completely terrified, but it a good way, like the anticipation right before getting on a rollercoaster. I'd only been to a theme park once in my life, but I still remembered the addicting rush of adrenaline.

I could easily imagine going to a theme park with Logan.

Or a haunted house.

Or bungee jumping.

Even the movies would probably be more fun with him. It would certainly go a lot better than my last date.

No. I needed to stop thinking like that.

Logan and I weren't dating, and I shouldn't put him in that position even in my imagination. It would be too easy to start to expect things from him.

Things I'd never get.

I didn't even know for certain if he was gay, though I had my suspicions based on the way he looked at me when I first showed up to his hotel room.

Gay or not, it didn't matter. We were on completely different levels. Friendship was already more than I could hope for, but he would never see me as anything else.

The seats inside the plane were upholstered with white leather, and the entire cockpit was spotless. It was such a pristine environment, and fit Logan perfectly.

I moved my hands from the arms of the chair to my lap and pinched them between my knees. Every place I touched inside the plane felt sullied. As if everything rotten inside me had leaked out and left a black stain behind.

I didn't belong here in this spotless environment, but Logan did. He deserved someone unsullied, and that could never be me.

We started rolling down the runway, quickly gaining speed until something seemed to tug just behind my solar plexus and the whole plane tipped upward. The ground disappeared from sight, and all I could see was an endless expanse of blue sky and white clouds stretching out in front of me.

There were so many different things in the plane Logan had to keep track of as we ascended, but he handled them with ease. It reminded me of an expert pianist who always knew exactly which key to hit to create grand music.

Only when the pressure behind my solar plexus disappeared and I didn't feel like I was being pressed back into my seat, did I dare to lean closer to the window and look down. The ground was so far away it looked like a patchwork quilt. I couldn't even comprehend what I was looking at for a moment, but soon I realized that the lines dissecting the patchwork landscape were roads, and the little dots moving along the line were cars.

Even the buildings, which from the ground created an entire city, merely looked like a collection of scattered Lego bricks.

"It's all so small," I marveled as I pressed my face against the glass. "I can't even see the people."

This high above the ground, it was like all of humanity ceased to exist except for the two of us. Everyone else was gone.

Something inside me snapped, like a tether that had been holding me to the ground had suddenly released and left me free-floating. I was completely untouchable up here. Everyone who'd ever hurt me, or failed me, or used me, was so far beneath me that they were invisible.

Flying above the world, I was untouchable. Even if one of the monsters from my past decided to show up again, they couldn't touch me if they tried.

"Clay?" Logan's hand on my shoulder turned me away from the window. "Are you okay?"

"What? Yeah, I'm fine."

With the back of one finger, he stroked my cheek, and when he pulled his hand away, a few drops of water clung to his skin.

At some point, while I'd been gazing at the world below, I'd started to cry without realizing. I wiped at my own cheeks, astonished at the tears I found there.

I'd cried plenty of times in my life. During my worst times it had been a daily occurrence, but I'd never cried like this before. Not only were the tears silent, but they didn't hurt. There was no rush of ugly emotion or flush of heat or pounding heart. I barely felt anything as a few more tears dripped from the corners of my eyes, except for a gentle sense of relief.

"Sorry," I said quickly as I wiped the new tears away. "I didn't realize. I'm not upset. I promise."

Luckily, he seemed to believe me, so I didn't have to explain the strange emotions I was feeling. I had no idea what to even call these emotions, let alone how to describe them, and I probably would have sounded like a lunatic if I tried.

The plane kept climbing, though the assent was much shallower than our initial takeoff, so I didn't feel the change as drastically. I didn't even realize we were still rising until we were engulfed within the clouds and came out on the other side above them. Now the world below us was completely gone, and only a landscape of clouds and sunlight remained.

"It looks like heaven."

Logan stared at me in shock. He tried to hide it, but I could tell I'd startled him.

I gave him a wide smile, instinctively tilting my head in a way that I knew showed off the angle of my jaw and the length of my neck in the best way.

"My therapist and I have been working on it. I still can't say…" The word *angel* tangled on my tongue, and I shook my head. "That word, but I've managed to conquer related terms. Pretty soon, it won't bother me at all."

"Good." Logan nodded. Something on the plane's controls changed, and he flipped a few switches before adjusting the position of the steering wheel—a U shaped thing that was apparently called the Yoke—so we were flying at a subtly different angle. "Although, it wouldn't matter even if you're never able to say that word again. The term doesn't really fit you anyway."

I watched him on the controls but couldn't understand what he was doing any more than I could understand what he was saying.

I wasn't an angel?

What did that mean?

I knew what I looked like. I was the stereotypical angel that appeared at the top of every Christmas tree and on every Hallmark greeting card. Even once I'd exchanged the round, cherubic cheeks of my youth for the sharper angles of adulthood, I could still have easily stared in a nativity play just by putting on a white robe.

Or did Logan mean it in a figurative sense?

Angels were considered to be pure beings, and I didn't fit that description anymore.

As if sensing the direction my thoughts had taken, Logan was quick to explain himself.

"I don't mean it in a bad way. I mean... here. Look."

He let go of the plane's yoke to fish his phone out of his pocket. I panicked at first, thinking we were about to crash, but Logan assured me that planes weren't the same as cars that needed constant steering. So long as we weren't altering our course, the autopilot could do most of the work.

He searched for something on his phone for a moment before handing it to me.

"This is what you reminded me of the first time we met."

It was a statue of an angel sitting in a particularly provocative pose, one hand on top of his head like he'd just pushed his shoulder length hair out of his face, and the cloth draped over his lap barely covering his otherwise naked form.

I glared at Logan. "Is this supposed to be some sort of joke?"

His cheeks flushed and he hurriedly scrolled down the page on his phone, nearly knocking it out of my hand in the process.

"No, I don't mean it like that. Ugh, I'm not explaining this well. Here. Read what it is."

Still trying to decide if I should be angry with him or not, I returned my gaze to the screen to read the description that the museum website had written below the picture.

It was called the *Genie du Maal,* and apparently it was a statue of Lucifer.

I scrolled back up to the image. What I had initially assumed to be typical angel wings were bare of all feathers. Instead, they had a membrane of skin and claws like a bat.

This was no angel. It was a demon.

Scrolling back down, I read the rest of the statue's description, and laughed out loud over the scandalous story of how it had come to be.

Handing him back his phone, I smirked at him. "So, when I showed up at your door, you thought I was the devil?"

Instead of putting his phone away, Logan tossed it into a cup holder near the yoke.

"You're certainly as tempting as the devil." He must not have meant to say that out loud, because he looked startled by the sound of his own words. He dropped his face into his hands, and groaned. "I'm sorry. That was inappropriate. I didn't mean—"

"Please don't," I interrupted him. One curious eye peeked at me from behind his hands, but Logan didn't raise his head. I couldn't look directly at him either. "Please don't say you didn't mean it. I..."

Should I say it?

Barely an hour ago I'd been scolding myself for daring to think of Logan in a romantic way, but that had been when we were on the ground. So far away from the rest of the world, all the things I'd been worried about seemed like they no longer mattered.

Gathering up my courage, I reached out and pulled his hands away from his face.

"I'd like it if you meant it." My cheeks were so flushed with embarrassment, I could feel heat radiating from them, but I pressed on. "I'd like it a lot."

His fingers slid between my own, one at a time like he was slowly weaving us together.

"Don't tell me that. You have no idea how hard it is being this close to you without kissing you. Fuck. I wanted to kiss you the first night we met, but I knew that wouldn't be appropriate."

I leaned forward until our foreheads touched. It was closer than we'd ever been before, but we still didn't cross that final line.

"Yeah, I wouldn't have responded well to that when we first met. Or, I'd have just assumed you were the same as everyone else and demanded that you pay for it."

I'd meant it as a joke, but the harsh reminder I'd just given myself made me jerk away from him.

For one precious moment, I'd forgotten my own past, but reality slammed back into me with the force of a sledgehammer against my brain.

"No. You can't mean this."

Logan let me pull back, but also refused to let go. He ended up leaning into my side of the cockpit, so he was awkwardly bent over the center armrest.

"Yes, I do mean it."

"Well, you shouldn't." I pressed against his shoulder but couldn't bear to truly shove him away. "You shouldn't want me. You deserve so much better. I can't give you any of my firsts. They've already been taken."

I was shouting now, but I couldn't stop. I gripped his shirt in a tight fist, pulling him closer. The thought of him leaving terrified me, even as I argued for that very outcome.

"You wouldn't be my first. You wouldn't even be my hundredth. I have nothing to offer you, and you deserve someone who can give you everything."

With every word I spoke, I pulled him closer until we were practically breathing the same air. My whole body trembled as Logan slowly raised his hands to cup either side of my face.

"I don't need everything. I just need you, because you are everything. Forget about society's stupid purity culture. It doesn't mean anything. Virginity is a made-up concept, anyway. Just answer me one question. Do you want to be with me?"

I nodded.

Of course I did.

What other answer could I give?

"Do you want me to kiss you?"

I nodded again.

"Then that's all that matters."

I opened my mouth to argue but found myself silenced when his lips pressed against mine.

It was a soft kiss. In my experience, kissing had always been rough and unpleasant, mostly focused on taking rather than giving, and often involved the use of more teeth than I was comfortable with.

This kiss was soft, and so different than what I'd known that I couldn't help melting against Logan with a pleased sigh.

Maybe I still had a few firsts to give him. Kissing Logan felt like nothing I'd ever experienced before, to the point that I wouldn't even dare put it in the same category of the kisses I'd been subjected to in the past.

I needed a new word. Logan's kiss, which filled me with such a sense of elation and seemed to tickle my very soul, deserved a name all its own.

We kissed until we ran out of air, then pulled back just enough to take a breath before kissing again. It would have gone on indefinitely if a beeping from the plane's controls hadn't caught our attention.

Logan returned to his place properly in the pilot's seat and took control of the plane again. Even just a few inches of space between us felt like too much. So, I hugged his arm against myself and curled up at his side as we continued on our flight, sneaking more, brief kisses every now and then.

For the first time in as long as I could remember, I was content. Eventually, we would have to come back down to earth, but I would have happily stayed up in the heavens forever.

CHAPTER TWENTY-FOUR

Logan

UNLIKE IN FAIRY tales or movies, true love's kiss did not magically solve all our problems.

Clay and I spent several days together while I waited to fly the social worker back home after the kids were settled into their new home. We spent most of the time indulging in cliché "date" activities, such as going to overly romantic restaurants, a fair, and even the movies.

We also traded plenty of other kisses, but never more than that. Clay clung to my shoulders and arms eagerly, but he seemed shy about touching anything beyond that, so I mimicked him. I knew from the moment we crossed the line into non-platonic territory that Clay would have to dictate the pace, and we could move as quickly or slowly as he wanted.

By the time I needed to leave to return to Baton Rouge, we had vaguely agreed to try long-distance for now, but nothing else. We would need to figure a lot more things out, but I had hope that we were at least on the right track.

Yet, I wasn't surprised when I arrived home to find I had several missed video calls from Clay. Throwing down my travel bag and collapsing on my bed, I took a deep breath and called him back.

"Hey, Clay. Something wrong? I noticed you called several times."

Clay answered the video call immediately, but he kept the phone at an angle so that it wasn't pointed directly at his face. I could still see his expression, so I knew something was off, but without being able to look directly into his eyes, I couldn't begin to guess what he was thinking.

"Logan. Sorry. I shouldn't have called so many times when I knew you were traveling. I just... panicked."

I sat up on the bed, ready to run out the door and all the way back to Maryland if necessary. "Panicked? Did something happen?"

"No." Clay finally looked directly at the screen, and I could see the red rims around his eyes that said he had been crying recently. "Nothing's wrong. I just got in my head after you left and started over-thinking things. But Jason was able to talk me down, so I'm fine now."

He laughed as if what he'd said was just a joke, but my own expression turned even more serious.

"Over-thinking about what? If you're having second thoughts, then—"

Clay cut me off before I could even finish the sentence.

"I'm not having second thoughts." He threw his hands out as if he meant to reach out to me, only to hit the cold surface of a screen instead. The phone was knocked off whatever he'd used to prop it up, and there were several moments of chaotic fumbling before I was able to see him again.

"I'm not having second thoughts," Clay repeated, looking more frazzled than before. Several strands of hair were stuck to his cheek, and I longed to reach out and tuck them behind his ears. "I'm having too many thoughts, is the problem. Until now, I never thought about having a real relationship with anyone. It didn't seem like something that was possible for me. Now that it is... I don't know what to think."

My first instinct was to immediately reassure him and tell him that everything was fine. We could take as long as he needed to figure things out, and if he ultimately did change his mind, then that would be okay, too.

However, then I took a closer look at him. He was twisting his fingers together, a certain sign that he was nervous, while also chewing on his bottom lip. This last action meant he had something he wanted to say, but he wasn't certain if he should speak up.

If I interrupted him now, he would swallow his words and bury them. So, as much as I wanted to speak, I kept my mouth shut and waited.

My patience was rewarded a moment later when, in a small breathless voice, Clay finally spoke.

"When you were here, all we did was

kiss. Relationships usually involve more than that."

With each word he spoke he looked more and more miserable.

Taking a chance, I spoke up. "A relationship doesn't have to include sex. You know that, right? Like... I love kissing you, and I'd be happy to do more, but it's also not a requirement. If kissing is all we ever do, I'll still be happy."

With a growl of frustration, Clay slammed his fist into the pillow beside him. "That's not the problem. I *want* to do more with you, but it's so confusing. I've never actually wanted anyone before. I've gotten so used to thinking of sex as something negative, something painful, that putting it together with you in my head feels wrong. Like I'm... making you dirty somehow by wanting you."

He sighed, and before I could even respond, he was already smoothing out the pillow and putting it back into place.

"Sorry. I've already talked about all this with Jason, so I know this way of thinking isn't right. I've already got an extra session with Doctor Coleman to help me work through it."

I was half-tempted to fly off back to

Maryland anyway, just so I could give him a hug. I hated to see Clay being so hard on himself.

Instead, I ran my finger over the screen, pretending the smooth surface under my skin was actually his cheek.

"It sounds like you're on the right track then. And I understand that this is all probably very confusing for you. Take as much time as you need to figure things out. I'm not going anywhere."

Blue eyes peered at me from under half-lowered lashes, and there was a playful glint back in Clay's eye as he pouted.

"But you did go somewhere. You're all the way over there in Louisiana while I'm stuck here, so many miles away. Long-distance relationships are hard. What if you get bored waiting for me, or find someone prettier?"

Based on his tone, he was mostly joking. Even if his words had a few real worries hidden in them, he was confident enough to turn them into a joke.

I laughed and shook my head, flashing him with a smile. "Is this your way of fishing for compliments? How could I possibly find someone prettier? You're already perfect."

Twirling a lock of hair around his finger, Clay started to bite his lip for a whole different reason. His actions were a bit stilted, like he wasn't sure what he was doing and was just going through the motions, but the distress he'd felt earlier had completely left his eyes and his posture was relaxed.

"Am I pretty enough for someone to make a statue of me?"

Apparently, Clay was amused by my comparison of him to the sexy statue of Lucifer. It had come up several times since our conversation in the plane. So much so, that it was becoming a running joke between us.

I shook my head, acting as if I was burdened by a great sorrow. "I'm afraid, if anyone tried to make a statue of you, it would be banned for being too distracting. Even keeping pictures of you on my phone is practically the same as carrying a concealed weapon." I smirked as I watched him struggle to contain his laughter. "Luckily, I've got a permit to conceal carry."

The dam broke, and Clay started laughing hard enough that he had to clutch his stomach to keep himself from falling over.

"Logan," he gasped through his laughter. "You're a total dork. You act all cool and badass, but you're actually just a weirdo."

His laughter caused me to laugh, until we were both howling.

"Oh no. My secret's been revealed. Now we'll have to stay together so I can make sure you never tell anyone."

It took a few minutes, but we eventually calmed down, and basked in the cathartic silence left behind after the outburst of positive emotions.

We sat so long in silence that I had no idea what time it was when Clay finally spoke up again.

"Thanks."

While we'd been enjoying the silence, I'd slumped back against my bed, and was already half asleep. I raised my head to get a better look at the screen, and the little shy smile on Clay's face made my heart stutter in my chest.

"For what?"

"For always knowing how to turn my craziness around into something positive. For taking everything so well. For just...

being you."

The miles between us felt so long and so small at the same time. It hadn't even been a day since I last saw him, and I already missed him so much, yet it also felt as though he were right there next to me.

"I'll keep being me if you keep being you. Deal?"

Clay's smile was so bright I feared it would burn out the screen of my phone.

"Deal."

CHAPTER TWENTY-FIVE

Logan

I SLAMMED THE door behind me so hard it rattled the wall. A dozen curses all welled up from my throat at the same time, and the only reason I didn't start shouting was because I didn't know which one to say first.

Every person in the office watched me with wide eyes and a silent mouth as I stomped over to my desk and collapsed into my chair. My head hit the solid top of my desk with an audible thunk, and I groaned into my own paperwork.

The noise of the FPA office slowly started up again, but I could tell just from the sound of people's footsteps that my coworkers were giving me a wide berth.

Eventually, a familiar pair of shoes stepped into my line of sight, and I looked up to see Roland standing beside my desk with an eyebrow raised and a concerned look on his face.

"Soooo, I take it your meeting with my brother didn't go well."

In was in moments like this when I regretted that my best friend and partner detective was also our Chief's younger brother. With anyone else, I could bitch about my boss without consequences. With Roland, I'd feel too guilty saying bad things about his own brother right to his face. Plus, he might end up revealing what I'd said to Mason. He wouldn't mean to, Roland would never snitch on me, but he was also a terrible liar and would likely end up saying something unintentionally.

"It went fine," I said through gritted teeth. "Those kidnappers we caught trying to abduct several kids were caught red-handed. We've got a watertight case against them. There's no question that they're going to jail."

Propping his hip against the corner of my desk, Roland physically hauled me up so I was sitting upright in my chair. "Then what's all this attitude about?"

"Those bastards haven't said a thing about who they're working for. They claim they were acting on their own, and apparently, there isn't enough evidence to prove otherwise. I wanted to hold off and continue pressing them, maybe offer them a better plea deal if they'll give us more info on the Bell ringers, but apparently the decision is out of my hands and above my pay grade. The higher-ups don't want to risk a surefire conviction for one that may or may not happen in the future. Never mind what keeps people the safest, right. Just go for what's easiest."

With another loud groan, I let my head drop back to the table.

Roland's hand thumped against my back a few times in a show of support. "Well, at least some of the bad guys are going behind bars, right. That's what we're here for after all."

My mouth pressed against the paperwork on my desk, muffling my voice. "Those guys are just lackies. Losing them won't even slow the Bell ringers down. Plus, how much will attempted kidnapping get? A few years? Soon enough, they'll be out and free to crawl back to their masters."

I didn't want to say it out loud, but the Bell ringer case wasn't going well.

We'd had one good success two months ago, when we set up the sting-operation and managed to catch some of the kidnappers and save multiple kids in one go.

Two months.

That should have been plenty of time to make more headway in the case, but after that night, all evidence of the Bell ringers had seemingly disappeared. Like pruning the limb of a tree, they had immediately erased all evidence of their access to home security systems, making it look like nothing had ever been amiss in the first place.

That wouldn't stop them, though. They had more than one way to get their hands on vulnerable kids. Without access to home security systems, they'd just rely more on altering adoption records in hospitals, like the case that Damien and Sebastian had brought down. Or any of the other "supply chains" they had set up for their human chattel.

The metaphor was overused, but I

couldn't help but think of the ancient Greek hero Hercules fighting the hydra. When we cut off one branch of the Bell ringers organization, more would just pop up.

Except, unlike with Hercules, we had no way to cauterize the wounds.

"What about your boyfriend?"

Roland's question had me sitting up so fast my chair tipped onto its two back legs.

"What're you talking about?"

Roland caught my chair before I topped over. "Clay Dahler. He's one of the Bell ringer's victims and was with them for years. We've already determined that there must be a lot of influential people backing the Bell ringers. Show him a list of possible suspects. Heck, show him a list of everyone who could possibly cover this kind of thing up. There are only so many people with that much power and resources. See if he recognizes anyone."

I slammed my hand down on the top of the desk, and several stacks of paperwork fell to the floor.

"No way. I'm not putting him through something like that. He's already told me everything he knows. Making him look through lists and lists of people, hoping he recognizes someone, will just stress him out for no reason. If he isn't able to help, he'll feel like he's failed, and the guilt will eat him up. And if he did recognize someone..."

I thought back to the multiple times I'd helped him while he broke down or talked him through a panic attack over the phone. He was getting better, but he wasn't free from his trauma. In the two months since the start of our relationship, he'd called me three times in the early hours of the morning when a nightmare had triggered a flashback, and he needed help finding his way back to reality.

"No," I said with even more conviction. "I could never put that kind of pressure on him. He's made so much progress, and I won't risk setting back his healing."

Sighing deeply, Roland bent down and retrieved my paperwork from the floor. "All right. Well, in that case, we may just have to accept that this is the best we're going to be able to achieve for now. Until more evidence is uncovered, there's not much we can do."

He was right. It aggravated every instinct I had until I nearly wanted to hiss like a cat whose fur had been rubbed the wrong way, but I had no argument for Roland.

This was the best we could do for now. It was just a shame that our best wasn't good enough.

CHAPTER TWENTY-SIX

Logan

MY PHONE STARTED ringing the second I stepped through the door of my apartment. It was Clay's ringtone, which I had recently changed to *Wind Beneath My Wings* in a moment when I'd been feeling particularly romantic, and although it was a bit sappy, it fit too well for me to consider changing it.

Clay knew when I got off work and must have calculated my commute down to the second to time his call so precisely. I pulled out my phone and answered the video call before I'd even sat down.

"Clay. I'm so glad to hear from you. It's

been a shit day."

"Well, hopefully I can make it better. Ooh, still in uniform. It really must have been a tough day. It took you longer to get home than usual."

I looked down at my clothes. It wasn't actually a uniform, just a business casual suit that was tailored enough to look professional, but comfortable enough for me to spend hours running around the city if I had to.

In a way, Clay wasn't wrong in calling it a uniform. I only wore such clothes when I was working, and usually preferred to wear jeans and a leather jacket when I was off the clock.

"Yeah," I sighed as I finally took a seat on my own couch. "A long day."

Should I tell him about the case?

I didn't want him to get involved, but he also deserved to know that the people who hurt him might never be brought to justice if we couldn't dig up more evidence.

I looked at his face, smiling eagerly at me through the screen. There was no way I could tell him about the Bell ringer case when he looked so happy. There was a spark of mischief in his eyes, and I knew he was in particularly high spirits. It would be cruel to ruin that with bleak news.

All thoughts of the Bell ringer case were pushed to the back of my mind, as far away from Clay as I could keep them.

Clay tugged at the collar of the bathrobe he was wearing. "Maybe I can cheer you up. Make your day a little better."

"My day's already better just hearing your voice."

"No, I mean..." He huffed and fidgeted with the collar of his bathrobe some more. "You'd think I'd be better at this, but I don't actually know how to get things started."

Based on his tone and expression, he was frustrated but not upset. Confused, I propped my phone up on some books on my coffee table so I could face it more directly and give Clay my full attention.

"What are you talking about? Get what started?"

Clasping his restless hands in his lap, Clay looked off to the side for a moment and took a deep breath, like he was gathering his strength, before turning back to me.

"Okay. So... Doctor Coleman had an idea."

"Your therapist?"

"Yeah. We've been working these last couple months on my hang ups around sex, and she had an idea to help me... ease into it."

Not sure where this was going, I just nodded and waited for him to explain.

Instead of words, he answered me with actions. He first set up the phone on the bookshelf across from his bed, then stepped back so that I was able to see all of him. The bathrobe covered him from wrist to ankle, which was odd since he usually wore his day clothes up until it was time to go to bed.

Unable to look directly at the screen, he toyed with the tie keeping the robe closed.

"Don't laugh if it looks stupid."

In one smooth motion, he removed his bathrobe. The cloth fell to the floor, and my jaw went with it.

Hidden under the robe was one of the sexiest sets of lingerie I'd ever seen. Not much of his skin was truly exposed, between the long velvet gloves that covered his arms, tall boots that reached to his mid-thigh, and the semi-transparent lace that showed off tantalizing peeks of his torso. Everything was in shades of red, making him look like a literal devil come to life.

"So?" Clay asked, tugging at the lace top to pull it down over his stomach as much as possible. "What do you think?"

My brain was still full of white noise, and my first several attempts at forming sentences came out as a stuttering mess.

"I— You— Clay— Fuck. You gotta warn a guy before hitting him with... all that."

Clay giggled as my tongue repeatedly tripped over itself, but there was a nervous edge to the sound that didn't sound entirely happy.

"So, you do like it?"

Finally getting myself back under control, I managed to piece my scattered brain back together and fully process what I was seeing.

"Of course I like it. But, Clay, what's all this about? You said this was Doctor Coleman's idea?"

"Well, not this specifically." He sat down on the edge of his bed, crossing his legs one over the other in a way that emphasized how good his limbs looked in the boots. "This outfit was my choice. That was the point. I've dressed up plenty of times for other people's pleasure, but I've never really chosen something simply because I like it. She suggested I pick out something that I liked and that made me feel good, as a way to... how did she put it... reclaim my agency when it comes to my sexuality."

"And nearly kill me in the process. You know, I was joking about you being pretty enough to be used as a weapon. You didn't need to make it literal."

This time Clay's laughter sounded a little more genuine. My positive reaction to his appearance seemed to help him feel more comfortable, and he was quickly gaining confidence in his flirting.

Leaning back on his arms so the lines of his body were on full display, he pointed at me with the toe of one boot.

"Looks like I'm not the only one packing a weapon."

I was so distracted by the sight of his legs encased in red leather that I didn't immediately notice what he was pointing at. My eyes trailed down him, from hip to toe, and only then did I follow the line of his leg toward myself.

And the very obvious tent in my pants.

Awkwardly clearing my throat, I crossed my legs in a useless effort to hide my reaction.

"Sorry. Don't worry about that."

"No. Don't hide." Clay uncrossed his legs and leaned forward so he was closer to the camera. "I've been working on getting more comfortable with combining the ideas of you and sex in my head. So, I don't want to shy away from it. I want to see."

"You want to see?" Clay's new position with his legs uncrossed gave me an even better view of his waist and inner thighs, which caused my erection to strain even harder against my pants. There was plenty for him to see, if that's what he wanted, but I wasn't certain what he was asking for.

Clay didn't seem to know either as he nervously bit at his thumbnail, then sputtered when he found himself biting velvet instead of his own skin and dropped his hand back down to his lap.

"Yeah, I want to see you." He toyed with the top of his boots and traced the seam that ran down his inner thigh in a way that was a tease I would have thought it was intentional if I didn't know better. "You've seen me undressed before. It's not fair that I've never seen you. Plus, I like the idea that you find me attractive. So... Let me see you. Please?"

The coy look he sent me from under his lashes was too intentional to be an accident. Maybe he did know what he was doing and was teasing me on purpose.

I certainly wasn't going to complain.

"All right." I shrugged and slipped off my jacket before unbuttoning my shirt. My actions were slow, taking my time on each button so that he could stop me if it turned out I'd misinterpreted his request.

My caution was unnecessary. The moment I started undressing, Clay perked up like an eager dog. If he had a tail, it would have started wagging.

"Really? You'll let me see?"

Removing my shirt, I tossed it aside, unconcerned with where it landed. "Were you expecting me to turn you down?"

His shy demeanor returned, and he ducked his head, but he never stopped looking me up and down. "I hoped you would agree, but I didn't know if you'd find doing something on camera like this uncomfortable."

Before removing my pants, I had to take my shoes off first. There was no sexy way to remove shoes, especially not ones with extra laces like mine, so I hurried through it to get them off as fast as possible.

"I told you before. We'll do whatever makes you comfortable. Does the distance between us help since I'm not actually in the room with you?"

Still eyeing me like I was putting on a fascinating show, Clay nodded. "I think so. If you were here with me that would probably be too much, but this is easier. I can make it stop just by turning off my phone."

With my hand on the button of my pants, I froze. "You know I would stop if you asked me to, right?"

"I know," Clay quickly reassured me. "But just because I know something is true, doesn't mean I feel it's true. That's a lot of what I've been working on with Doctor Coleman. Everything involving sex feels like a threat, even when I know it's safe. That's why this is a good starting point. The threat is minimal since you're so far away."

At first, I felt insulted that Clay considered me a threat, but I kept my mouth closed and breathed through my nose as I let the hurt from his words wash past me. It was one of the first things they reiterated to us when I joined the FPA, to evaluate our reactions and not let our own emotions affect the way we treated people.

It was a hard lesson to remember in the heat of the moment and required the discipline of all my years on the police force.

Clay didn't mean to insult me. He was just explaining his mindset and he trusted me enough not to misinterpret or take it personally.

After reminding myself of this, the sting of his accusation faded, and my heart was calm once again.

"So, you want me to continue?"

With an eager smile on his face, Clay braced his elbow on his knee and propped his chin in his hand to stare at me expectantly.

"Yes, please."

Despite my earlier confidence, I'd never actually stripped on camera. There was something more vulnerable about it than when my partner was in the room with me. It wasn't a bad feeling, but I did feel like I was on display.

Since I was sitting down, there was no choice but to stand up so I could remove my pants. The way I had my phone angled meant that the upper half of my body was off the screen when I was standing, so Clay was really getting a full view of everything he wanted to see.

At least he seemed to be enjoying the show, based on the sparkle in his eyes as he watched me.

Taking a deep breath, I pushed my pants off my hips and let them fall to the floor. Then, before I could lose my nerve, I shoved my underwear off just as quickly.

When I sat back down, the leather material of my couch was cold against my skin, yet I felt hotter than ever. My arousal hadn't dimmed at all since Clay first revealed his outfit. If anything, the embarrassment crawling under my skin only made me even harder. That was something I hadn't known about myself, and blood rushed to my cheeks as I blushed.

Trying to adopt a relaxed pose, like I wasn't screaming on the inside, I threw an arm over the back of my couch.

"Good?"

I had no idea what I was even asking about.

Was I good?

Was he good?

I just needed to say something to fill the silence, and it was the only thing I could think of saying.

Clay didn't seem to mind as he bit his lip and drank me in with his eyes. "Hmm. Very good."

Still wanting to go at his speed, I didn't make another move despite the erection that was now throbbing painfully hard between my legs.

"What do you want me to do now?"

"What?" Clay looked up at me, meeting my eyes for the first time in several minutes with a startled expression.

"Come on," I encouraged. "This is your show. So, tell me what you want me to do next. I'm following your command."

"Really? Anything?" He was obviously intrigued by the idea, but also skeptical as his eyes narrowed at me. "What if I wanted you to start doing jumping jacks?"

Without hesitation, I stood from the couch intending to follow his orders, but he stopped me before I could get started.

"Wait. Stop. Come back. I don't actually want you to do that."

I sat back down, this time throwing both arms over the back of the couch so that I was lounging more than sitting.

"So, what do you want me to do? Give me the word and I'll do it."

Clay gaped at me, eyes alight with possibilities, but also in complete disbelief that he was being given such an opportunity.

The bottom part of his outfit was made of velvet just like his gloves. Calling them shorts was a generous term, since they didn't cover his legs at all, but the thicker material hid his body more than typical lingerie. Until now, there had been no hint of actual arousal from him, but he must have found the idea of ordering me around very appealing, because a noticeable tent formed in the front of his shorts.

The evidence of his arousal helped ease my own embarrassment. I must be doing something right if Clay found it so exciting.

While I'd been distracted observing him, he'd been busy deciding what to do with his newfound power. He sat up straighter, as if his bed were a throne, and gave me a look like a king regarding his loyal subject.

"You told me before that you've had dreams about me. I want to see how you take care of yourself after these dreams."

What could a subject do but obey his king?

With the real thing sitting right in front of me, it wasn't hard to remember how my dreams of him would leave me a sweating, desperate mess. I already ached for him, and now that I had permission, my hand found my cock as if it had been magnetized. I immediately started stroking myself, moaning as pleasure licked up my spine like fire, and squeezed my eyes shut tight.

"Stop."

My hand froze the moment I heard Clay's order, and my head fell back against the couch with a groan of frustration.

"Clay. You're killing me."

He laughed at me, and although I was practically writhing with desperation, I smiled as well.

"You're going too fast," he chastised

me, shaking his head like I'd disappointed him. "I want you to go slower so I can enjoy it."

I could already see his plan forming behind his eyes. He was going to tease me for as long as he could. The power I'd given him over me excited him, and he planned to make it last.

Bracing myself for a rough ride, I followed his request and started stroking myself much slower than before.

It was torture. I wanted nothing more than to take myself firmly in hand and chase the orgasm that was building in my gut, but Clay wouldn't let me. He insisted that I keep my touch slow and soft, and even started directing me on exactly how I should touch myself.

For a full minute, he had me focus on just the head of my cock, bringing myself so close to orgasm my vision started to turn white. Then, just before I found release, he ordered my hands away from my cock entirely and only let me touch my thighs and chest until I calmed down. Then, when I could finally touch my cock again, I had to keep my strokes so light and slow that I could barely feel them.

It was the most intense kind of edging

because I was doing it to myself. At any moment, I could easily put an end to it and let myself come, but my hands seemed to no longer be connected to me. They moved only under Clay's command, as if he'd somehow reached into my brain and taken direct control of me.

Clay never took his own clothes off, but at some point, he started rubbing himself through his shorts. I couldn't even enjoy the sight of him pleasuring himself, trapped as I was within the prison of my own skin. He controlled everything. He told me when I could make noise and when I had to be silent. When I could close my eyes and when I had to keep them open.

I obeyed every word he said.

The sun was still up when I returned home from work, but it had set behind the horizon when Clay finally gave me permission to finish. Tears were leaking from my eyes at that point, and it didn't take more than a couple of quick strokes for me to fall over the edge that I'd been teetering on for so long.

My throat was a dry, tangled knot, and the moan that I let out when I came sounded like someone was choking me. I made a mess of my own hand and thighs, and even managed to stain the couch, but I didn't care about the cleanup. My brain was filled with nothing but static and fog as I lay sprawled over the couch, as limp as a wet rag.

"Wow," Clay gasped. His voice was breathless, and when I cracked one eye open to look at him, I could see a wet patch on the front of his shorts.

I tried to sit up, but my boneless limbs wouldn't cooperate, and I collapsed back into my undignified sprawl.

"Forget what I said earlier. You weren't trying to kill me before. This is how you plan on killing me."

Clay's whole body was shaking, though I suspected it was more from emotional exhaustion than physical exertion. He lay down sideways on his bed, using his arms as a pillow so he could still look at the phone. "That would be such a waste. I've got too many plans to kill you now."

I groaned again and ran my clean hand through my sweaty hair to push it out of my eyes.

"Fuck. If that's what sex is like when you're seven states away, I don't think I could handle having you in the same room."

Clay scowled at me, his pale eyebrows furrowing, but it was clearly a joke since his lips were still smiling.

"You'd better figure out how to handle it, because that's my goal. Someday we're going to have sex for real, and you better be ready when we do."

The half-assed salute I gave him would have horrified my drill instructors from the past.

"Sir, yes, sir. I promise, I will rise to the occasion."

Clay smothered his giggle against his arms, but I could still hear him. Every time I heard him laugh it made my heart nearly float out of my chest.

When we first met, such sounds of joy seemed impossible for him. He'd come such a long way in such a relatively short amount of time.

The memory of my early conversation with Roland flickered to life in my mind, but I immediately pushed it away. There were so many things I could talk to Clay about, but I would not be bringing up the Bell ringer case. Especially not now, after we just made another monumental leap forward in our relationship.

Maybe, someday, I'd bring it up with him, but today was not that day.

In fact, that day might never come, but as I listened to Clay's laughter, I realized that failing to solve the Bell ringer case wouldn't be the end of the world. I wouldn't give up on it, but I also had to admit when something was beyond me.

I couldn't solve this case all by myself, but I could dedicate myself to ensuring Clay's happiness, and help him keep moving forward.

Even if that was all I ended up achieving, it would be enough.

CHAPTER TWENTY-SEVEN

Clay

MY EYES ITCHED with fatigue, and the numbers on the page were swimming on front of me, but I refused to put the book down.

It was already past midnight. I'd been studying for nearly six hours and my brain felt like it was about to explode and leak out of my ears.

How did teenagers manage to study all this stuff?

I was an adult. I should be able to keep up with children, but the longer I stared at the textbook, the stupider I felt.

The door to my bedroom swung open

with a slow creak. By now, I could recognize the difference between Jason and Patrick's footsteps, so I didn't bother to look up as my brother approached me.

"Clay. You're still studying?"

Dropping the book onto the table, I pressed my face against its pages, so my nose buried right into the crease of the binding and filled my senses with the smell of paper.

"Studying is the wrong word. More like staring blankly in confusion. Everything's just running together in my brain."

Lifting my head up enough to pull the book out from under it, Jason started to put it back with the rest of my study supplies.

"You need to take a break for today. It'll still be here for you tomorrow."

I pulled the book out of his hands but didn't have the heart to open it again. "I can't quit. I need to keep going. I'm not good enough yet."

Before Jason could even ask, I handed him a paper that had been stuffed at the bottom of the stack of textbooks.

"Another practice GED test. Didn't you just take one?"

"Yes, but I've been studying a lot so I

thought maybe this time it would be better, but it was even worse."

With precise movements, Clay folded the paper into a small square, so it resembled an accordion. "Of course you're not going to do well when you're stressing yourself out about it. You need to take a break."

"No, it's not enough. I still didn't pass. Children can pass this thing, but I can't."

Jason flicked the folded paper at me, and it bounced off my nose. "First of all, high school seniors aren't that much younger than you. Stop talking like you're an old man. And secondly, it's only been a year and a half since you moved here. Less than that since you started tutoring. You're trying to cram years of schooling into a matter of months. Don't be so hard on yourself. Besides, what's the rush?"

I tipped my head to the side, just enough to free my mouth. "I talked with Logan earlier. He's getting a promotion at work."

My room only had one chair, so there was nowhere else for Jason to sit. This didn't stop him as he knelt right on the floor next to my desk and placed a hand on my arm.

"That's... good, right?"

"Yeah." I sat up, but my posture remained slouched, so although Jason was kneeling next to me, our heads were nearly the same height. "He's going to be running his own task force. I know he's excited about it."

I also knew that his promotion had to do with the Bell ringer case. Logan never talked about the case, but I could piece the puzzle together. He worked for a department that specialized in crimes against children. He'd specifically been sent to find me, and I'd even seen him writing down information about my kidnappers. Add to that the kids that he'd brought to Dominic's place that had nearly been kidnapped by traffickers, and that lead to one conclusion.

He was still trying to bring down the pedophile ring that had abused me. The case was apparently important enough to require its own task force, and now Logan was in charge of that task force.

Or maybe he was in charge of one branch of the task force?

I didn't know how these things worked.

I didn't know a lot of things, and the more I learned, the more I realized how much I didn't know.

I kept all this information to myself, and only told Jason about the most pressing issue.

"Logan's moving forward in his career. He's building a future for himself, and... I don't know where I fit into that future. I've got nothing. No education. No job—and don't you try to argue with me, Jason. You and I both know the work I do for your company isn't worth the amount that you pay me. That doesn't count as a real job."

Jason's mouth closed with an audible snap. He scowled, clearly still wanting to dispute what I'd said, but he let me talk.

"I don't even know what I want to do with my future, but getting my GED is at least a place to start. I just feel like, if I don't hurry, then I'll never be able to catch up with Logan, and his life is going to move on without me."

Gripping my hands, Jason pulled me away from the desk until I was forced to join him on the floor. He was taller than me, though not by much, and when I leaned against his side, we were in almost perfect alignment.

"Clay, you said it yourself that you

don't know what you want for your future. Maybe you have a future with Logan, maybe you don't. If he's as good a man as he seems, then he'll wait for you, and if he isn't willing to wait for you, then he's not the right person for you anyway. So don't run yourself ragged trying to chase after him."

I huffed and let my head rest against his shoulder. "It's not that I don't think he'd wait. He's been so good about being patient, even though I know our relationship is hard for him. Long-distance is difficult enough, but with all my issues on top of it, most people would have already walked away by now."

Although I wasn't looking at him, I could feel my brother about to argue, so I raised a hand to cut him off.

"I know my issues aren't my fault, and that there's nothing wrong with them. Trust me, I've been over that so many times with Doctor Coleman. But you can't say I don't have issues. The very fact that I'm studying for my GED at the age of twenty-four is proof of that."

Pulling me closer, Jason pressed a kiss to the top of my head. "As long as you know that you're just fine the way you are, then I won't argue."

I shrugged off the intimate gesture, but didn't pull away from him, which was proof of the progress I'd already made. A year and a half ago, I never would have let him so close.

"I wouldn't use the word 'fine' but I get your point. What I'm trying to say is that I don't think Logan is going to leave me. If anything, I'm worried that he'll stick around too long. I don't want to be an anchor dragging him down. I already feel guilty enough about everything you've done for me. If Logan ended up having to sacrifice for me as well, I think that would be too much to handle."

Jason took a while to respond. As I waited for him to gather his words, my eyelids drooped, and my exhaustion began to catch up to me. I was just contemplating closing my eyes when Jason finally spoke up.

"We've already talked about the so-called 'sacrifices' I've made for you, so I'm not going to rehash that conversation. Instead, I'll just say that I understand your concerns. You want to make something of yourself and be a worthy partner for the person you care about.

Trust me. I get that. For the first few years of our relationship, I didn't feel worthy of Patrick. I was putting all of my energy into finding you that I felt like I was just dragging him down. I even almost broke up with him."

"What?" My gasp was louder than I intended, turning into more of a shout as I shoved his shoulder to make him face me. "You never told me that."

Jason just looked sheepish and shrugged. "I didn't want you to feel guilty about something that didn't happen. We never actually broke up, so there was no reason for you to worry about it. I'm just saying that I get where you're coming from. It's hard when you feel like you're not equal to our partner, but when I suggested breaking up to Patrick, you know what he said to me?"

The question was obviously rhetorical, but I couldn't help shaking my head in response.

Jason laughed with a melancholy little puff of air.

"He said that my tenacity to keep looking for you no matter what was one of the things that attracted him to me in the first place, and he refused to let our relationship end over the very thing that had brought us together. I realized then that, just because I saw something in a negative light, didn't mean that Patrick saw it the same way."

In an unexpected move, Jason ruffled my hair as if I were still a little kid. I slapped his hand away and smoothed my hair back into place. We both knew I wasn't really upset, but I still had my dignity to maintain.

Jason wasn't deterred and messed up my hair again anyway.

"You should talk to Logan about this. Not just about studying for the GED, but about everything. How you feel unequal in the relationship, your worries for the future. Everything. The real thing that moves a relationship forward is communication."

"All right," I said as I stifled a yawn behind my hand. "I'll talk to him. Eventually. I don't want to rain on his parade right after he just got a promotion."

"Fair enough." Jason stood, and after brushing the imaginary dust from his knees, he pulled my arm to help me up as well. "Now, come on. It's late, and you look like you're about to fall asleep right there on the floor. Your bed will be much more comfortable."

I stumbled my way through my nightly routine, brushing my teeth and changing into pajamas, before falling into bed. I fell asleep almost as soon as my head hit the pillow, but the textbooks waiting for me on my desk haunted me in my dreams.

Like something straight out of a Harry Potter movie, I dreamed of books with teeth skittering over the floor and snapping at my ankles. I couldn't even see where I was running to. The path I walked had no end. Yet, with each step I took I felt like I was falling farther and farther behind.

CHAPTER TWENTY-EIGHT

Clay

WITH JASON'S SUGGESTION in mind, I took a break from studying the next day to call Logan earlier than normal. It was Saturday, and he had the day off, so I got up early to call him around the time he usually woke up.

As expected, he answered my call right away.

"Clay. You don't usually call this early. Is something wrong?"

His voice was rough and heavy with sleep. The sound of it sent a pleasant shiver up my spine. I could easily imagine waking up to that voice every day, but I was getting ahead of myself. We still lived in separate states and hadn't even slept together properly yet. It was too soon for me to be thinking about the rest of our lives.

"I just wanted to make your morning a little better."

I could see on the screen of the video call that he was still in bed. His hair was a mess, and the sheets were tangled around him. He must have immediately reached for the phone when he heard the ring and not even bothered to sit up first.

The smile he gave me was soft and warm. "Getting to hear your voice when I first wake up already makes this a great morning. Hopefully, I'll eventually be able to wake up like this every morning."

Apparently, I wasn't the only one who was thinking about 'the rest of our lives'. As soon as he realized what he'd said, Logan looked embarrassed, but didn't try to take back his statement.

I didn't draw attention to it either.

"So, did you have any good dreams about me?"

Logan choked on nothing and started violently coughing. From that reaction alone, I suspected the answer was "yes".

LOGAN

Then, when he reached for a glass of water sitting on his bedside table, the bed sheets shifted and revealed an obvious tent in his pajama pants.

Now I knew I was right. He had dreamed about me.

It had been four months since our relationship turned sexual, though everything was still done long-distance over video-calls. I was getting used to it and was no longer wracked with guilt and confusion every time I found him attractive.

Just the thought of some phantom version of me visiting him in his dreams sparked my own arousal.

"Looks like I was right. You did dream about me. I can help you with that."

Looking down at himself, Logan didn't bother trying to hide his arousal. It was too obvious.

Though he still blushed.

"What did you have in mind?"

His voice was even rougher than a moment ago.

I wanted to hear him moan with that gravelly voice.

"First, get rid of those pants. They aren't hiding anything."

He immediately did as I said, and I was soon greeted by the image of him lying naked across his bed.

I glanced toward my own bedroom door, double-checking that I'd turned the lock. We would all be humiliated if Jason or Patrick interrupted us.

Whenever our 'video dates' turned sexual, I was usually the one to call the shots. I found a lot of pleasure in getting to be the one giving the orders for once, and Logan definitely enjoyed it as well.

This time was no different.

My breath caught in my lungs as I watched his hand slide down his stomach before curling around his cock.

"Tell me about your dream."

His hand stuttered and he lost the rhythm of his strokes.

"What? Now?"

"Yes, now. Keep going, but also tell me what you dreamed about."

His hand started moving over himself again, but his strokes weren't as smooth as they'd been before.

"You were sitting on some sort of throne."

"Oh?" I already liked where this dream was going, and I slipped my own hand inside my pants.

Logan's eyes squeezed closed, and his hand sped up a little more as he fully fell into the memory of the dream. "Yeah. I was kneeling in front of you, and you…" He gasped, and his face burned such a bright red I was afraid his bed sheets were about to catch fire.

"Go on," I encouraged when he didn't continue. "What was I doing?"

The hand that wasn't on his cock clamped over his mouth like he wanted to silence himself, but we'd already learned that he couldn't resist when I gave him a direct order, and moment later he was talking again.

"You were holding onto a chain that was attached to my neck."

"Ooh, kinky." My own cock was demanding attention now, and I started stroking it in time to Logan's movements. "Is that the kind of stuff you like?"

"I didn't used to." He moaned as pre-come began to coat the head of his cock, then turned his head to look directly at me. "The devil made me do it."

He knew how much I liked it whenever he compared me to demonic imagery. It was so different from all the things I'd been called in the past and felt like I was forging a new identity.

I bit my lip as my legs squirmed under my sheets. "So, I've got you chained and kneeling at my feet. Then what do I do with you?"

"You-you... I don't know."

"Yes, you do," I insisted. "Tell me. What did I do with you?"

Logan didn't usually put up any protest to my orders. For him to deny me now meant that the dream must have been particularly embarrassing.

That only made me more eager for the answer.

"You..." He hesitated one last time before giving in. "You were wearing these really tall boots, and you made me unzip them with my teeth."

Just the memory of the dream was enough for his cock to visibly throb in his hand. I knew he liked the way my legs looked in the tall boots I'd worn before, but I hadn't realized how much.

I still had those boots. I'd have to get them out again for another video date.

"Was that it? I just made you take off my boots."

He was too overcome by the pleasure

running through him to talk anymore. All he could do was shake his head and mumble a few incoherent words.

I was also on the verge of losing my own composure and gripped my cock a little tighter to try and calm myself down.

"Come on, Logan. Tell me. What did I do next?"

The rest of the dream all came out in one long ramble as Logan started to stroke himself even faster.

"You made me kiss all the way up each leg, from ankle to hip. I wasn't allowed to miss a single inch of skin or else I'd have to start all over again."

I couldn't help it. I laughed out loud, even as my own orgasm was quickly approaching.

"You really do like my legs, huh?"

He just bit his lip and nodded.

"Then what happened?"

"I don't know," he shouted. This time his denial didn't sound like embarrassment, but frustration. "I never found out what happened next. That's when I woke up."

"Ugh, really?" My back arched as a particularly strong wave of pleasure washed over me. "We didn't even get to the good stuff. Well, I can fix that. Close your eyes and picture your dream."

He did, and I could tell he was close just from the breathy little sounds he made.

"Imagine, after you finish with the second leg, I hook it around the back of your neck and pull you closer."

He groaned, clearly liking the image I was painting.

"I grip your head with both my hands and draw you up into a firm kiss. It steals the air right out of your lungs, and you're left panting. Then, before you can catch your breath, I shove your head down between my legs and tell you to get to work."

That was all it took. Almost as soon as the words left my mouth, Logan's back arched drastically off the bed, and he came with a strangled shout. The sight of him, literally writhing in the throes of his orgasm, drove me over the edge as well. I buried my face against my pillow as I came into my own hand, desperately hoping the walls of Jason's house were thick enough to block the sound.

Logan and I lay in our respective beds, over a thousand miles apart. Not for the first time, I wished I could reach through the screen and wrap myself around him. His scent and the feel of his skin already felt like distant memories, and my heart ached over the empty place at my side where he should have been.

"Damn, baby," Logan gasped when he could talk again. "Just when I think you can't surprise me anymore, you prove me wrong."

"That should be my line. I didn't know you were into the kinky stuff."

He was still so flushed from his recent orgasm that it hid his embarrassment. "I didn't used to be like this. You just bring it out of me."

Even just a few months ago, I would have worried that I was somehow corrupting him, but now I took it as a compliment. Logan wanted me so much that his very sexuality was warming to accommodate his desire.

After we'd calmed down, we talked for a few minutes before eventually hanging up. I promised to call him later, but I wanted to spend a few hours volunteering at Dominic's place now that I had a free day.

After showering and getting dressed, I

headed downstairs to find Jason and Patrick both in the living room watching the morning news on the television.

"So," Jason said as soon as I stepped into the room. "You and Logan talked?"

His grin was so smug, there was no question that he knew what we'd done.

Damn his house's thin walls.

I just grinned back at him. "Yeah. We talked."

Patrick said something, probably chastising Jason for teasing me, but I never heard what he said.

At that moment, I happened to glance at the news story playing out on the television and my whole world froze. A man stood on a very official looking podium, talking to a bunch of news reporters, while a small group gathered around behind him. I couldn't tell what they were talking about, but everyone wore solemn expressions.

One person among the group stood out to me in particular, standing just behind the person talking.

That face.

I knew that face.

Someone started screaming, and I bit my lip until it bled. Our captors hated it when we screamed, so I'd learned to keep myself quiet.

Hands reaching everywhere.

Tugging.

Pulling.

Always hurting.

I needed to stay quiet, or it would just hurt more. Some kids learned that lesson, and some never did. The ones who didn't learn, didn't survive.

I was good.

I was smart.

I stayed quiet, so I would live.

All the while, that familiar face hung in my vision. The expression was always somber, even when it was laughing at me.

Even when it hurt.

No, wait.

I was in Jason's house. There was no reason to stay quiet now. If I wanted to scream, I could scream.

I tried, but there was suddenly no air in the room, and I clawed at my own throat as I tried to breathe.

How were Jason and Patrick breathing when there was no air?

Everything around me went dark. This wasn't the same as slipping into the Midnight Zone. When I was in the

Midnight Zone, it was always pleasant. I felt nothing and wasn't even aware of my own body.

This was the exact opposite. I was hyperaware of my body, as if the very blood in my veins had been replaced by barbed wire.

Other people were screaming now. It wasn't fair.

Why were they allowed to scream when I had to remain silent?

I wanted to scream too, but there was no air and I couldn't make a sound.

The last thing I felt was pain in my knees as they hit the floor.

CHAPTER TWENTY-NINE

Logan

THE FLIGHT FROM Baton Rouge, Louisiana to Kent Island, Maryland usually took a little over two hours. I did it in seventy minutes. I probably broke several air traffic laws to get there so quickly, but I didn't care.

When Jason Dahler called me to say that Clay was in the hospital, my heart stopped beating, and it didn't start again until I laid eyes on him myself.

"A panic attack," the doctor's said. They'd put him on some heavy sedatives to calm him down, but he should wake up soon.

Everyone acted as if it were normal. As if keeping a perfectly healthy man unconscious so his body wouldn't turn against itself out of fear was a completely ordinary thing.

I counted each rise and fall of Clay's chest as I sat beside the bed.

"What happened?"

Jason, who sat on the other side of Clay's hospital bed with a worried expression that matched my own, took a minute to respond.

"I'm not sure. He got up later than usual this morning. When he eventually came downstairs, he took one step into the living room and just froze there with this look of horror on his face. Then he collapsed."

The fact that Jason didn't question why Clay had gotten up late meant that he already knew exactly what his brother and I had been doing over video call. My face grew hot, but my expression stayed neutral as I demanded a detailed description of the moments right before Clay collapsed. Jason painted a clear picture, picking apart every detail of the room around them and every word they exchanged right up until the tragic moment.

"You said you were watching the news on TV?"

Jason thought for a moment. "Patrick was watching it. I wasn't really paying attention, so I don't know what it was talking about. Is it important?"

I leaned back in my chair and rubbed at my gritty, tired eyes. It felt like I hadn't blinked since getting Jason's call.

"Whatever was playing on the news is the only unknown variable of the situation, so let's start there. Ask Patrick if he remembers what was being shown."

A few minutes and one phone call later, we had our answer.

It was a press conference about the recent joint effort to "clean up" the country and put a stop to the human trafficking that was plaguing many states more than ever before. No one wanted to admit that the amount of trafficking hadn't increased, the Bell ringer case had just made us more aware of it. However, hard truths like that didn't reassure the public.

I'd been consulted for that press conference. I knew many of the people who appeared in that news story. If the sight of one of them triggered Clay's panic attack, there was only reason I could think of.

We already suspected that powerful people must be behind the Bell ringers. I just never expected them to show up so close to home.

But which one?

There were many people at the press conference. Any one of them could have been what set Clay off. I itched under my skin with the need to find the people who hurt Clay and get rid of them, assure that they could never hurt anyone else, but I was helpless until I knew the identity of my target.

Silently, Jason and I shared a look, and I could see in his eyes the same desire that ran through my veins. When I finally began my crusade against this monster, I would have another ally.

On the bed between us, Clay stirred. Pale lashes fluttered open, revealing a familiar shade of blue that always took my breath away. His gaze was blurry, unfocused, but he quickly regained his wits when he saw Jason and I beside him.

"Fuck."

That was it. No questions about what

happened, where he was, or how he got there. Just radical acceptance of his situation, and a complete lack of surprise.

Taking a deep breath, he sat up just enough to look at Jason and I a little more directly. "I don't suppose you'll agree to just ignore what happened?"

Jason grabbed Clay's hand, which sat limply on the bed. "Clay. You had a major panic attack. What…"

He didn't bother finishing the question. All of us already knew the answer.

I grabbed Clay's other hand.

"Who was it?"

For a moment, it looked like he was going to play dumb and pretend he had no idea what I was talking about. I could see the lies building up in his eyes. However, he deflated before he could say a word and sighed as he resigned himself to the truth.

When we first met, he would have lied to me without hesitation. Despite the situation, I couldn't help the little spark of pride that I felt witnessing the evidence of how much he'd healed since then.

Clay didn't meet either his brother's eyes or mine as he picked at the tape holding his IV in place.

"I don't know who it was. I just recognized the face. It was... it was one of the men in charge of the Bell ringers. I remember him because, every time he showed up, he always wanted to... 'inspect the product'. Those days were some of the worst."

He managed to peel most of the tape up, and I stopped him before he accidentally removed the IV.

Something wet landed on the back of my hand, and I looked up to see Clay crying. It wasn't the first time I'd seen him cry, but these tears were different. They were completely silent, and he made almost no expression at all while water fell one drop at a time from his eyes as if he were leaking.

"Sorry." Clay wiped the tears away and shook himself, banishing whatever memories had risen behind his eyes. "The worst part wasn't his visits. It was the anticipation. We always knew when the 'special guest' was coming because our keepers would start treating us extra well during the days leading up, to make sure we were in good condition. We would know he was coming, but we wouldn't know when."

My heart stuttered, like someone had reached into my chest and squeezed, as another piece of Clay's puzzle fell into place. For years, being treated well was a warning that more suffering was coming. It was no wonder he struggled so hard to trust people and accept kindness.

If I were him, I don't think I'd ever be able to trust anyone again. The fact that he could was a testament to Clay's strength.

In that moment, I would have fallen in love with him if I wasn't already.

I wished that I could end the conversation there and let the memories fade away, but I couldn't. Hating myself for what I was about to do, I pulled out my phone and started searching for the press conference that had aired earlier.

"Clay, I hate asking this of you, but—"

He cut me off by placing a hand on my knee.

"You need me to identify him."

"Now hold on." Jason stood from his seat, puffing up like he was about to storm around the bed and attack me. "Clay passed out just from seeing this person's face. You can't make him go through that again. Not after he just woke up."

Clay tugged at Jason's sleeve, urging his brother to sit back down.

"Jason. It's okay. I get it. In fact, I think... I think I want to do it."

Jason sat down slowly, though he was still glaring at me.

"Really? You're not just saying that. You know, you aren't obligated to put yourself at risk."

Clay's hair was a mess, and it became even more tangled as he rapidly shook his head. "No. I want to. No one... no one else should have to go through what I did. I if I can help put a stop to it, then I want to do it."

When his brother still didn't look convinced, Clay turned to me, clutching my sleeve and staring at me with beseeching eyes.

"Logan. Please. I'll be fine. I promise. It was such a shock before because I didn't expect it and I wasn't ready. This time I'll know what I'm about to see, so I won't panic. I want to help. Please."

He already had me on the first please. By the second one, I was ready to hand over anything he wanted.

"All right," I relented.

Of course I did.

What other choice was there when he looked at me with such emotion in his blue eyes?

"I'm not going to play the video, but just take a look at this picture and tell me which face is familiar."

I handed over my phone, trying not to visibly flinch as I waited for the outcome.

Clay stared at it for a while. At first, I thought maybe we were wrong, and he didn't recognize anyone. While I wanted answers, I was also relieved by the idea of not having to put Clay through any more stress.

Then Clay zoomed in on the picture so only one face was visible and handed the phone back to me.

"That's him."

His voice cracked, and I could feel his hands shaking when I took the phone from him. It wasn't a panic attack, but he was clearly still affected.

Jason wrapped an arm around Clay's shoulders and started talking to him in a low, soothing voice. He'd been present for more of Clay's panic attacks and emotional episodes than I had, and obviously knew what to do during these moments. So, I let the brothers have their moment undisturbed as I looked down at the phone in my hands.

It took me a few seconds to comprehend what I was seeing. The face that stared up at me wasn't the one I expected.

Preston Vanshaw.

The assistant director of the FBI.

Just before Alias Investigations had asked me to look into Clay's case, they'd run into their own trouble that had resulted in the death of the FBI director. There had been a big reshuffling of power in the FBI, and many people's jobs had been in jeopardy.

Preston Vanshaw, however, was one of the few who'd seemingly been immune to the change in power. His position now was just as secure as it had been a few years ago.

This man was a few years younger than me.

How could he have anything to do with what happened to Clay?

Then I remembered that Vanshaw was a trust-fund baby who'd only gotten his position because his father held the position of assistant FBI director before him. He was an example of nepotism at its finest.

A picture began to form in my mind. Vanshaw hadn't even been born when the Bell ringers first started operating, so he obviously hadn't started the whole thing.

Was this some sort of messed up inheritance?

He'd not only been handed a powerful career, but also inherited a lucrative trafficking business.

If that was the case, it was no wonder he viewed the children they'd kidnapped as a commodity. He'd probably been raised to that mindset from the moment he was born.

I would have almost pitied the man, if he hadn't personally contributed to hurting Clay. As it was, I only pitied what was going to happen to the bastard when I got my hands on him.

It took a few minutes for Jason to calm Clay down. By that time, a nurse came into the room to check over Clay now that he was awake. Jason and I were asked to step out of the room so she could speak with Clay privately.

I'd been through similar situations enough to know better than to argue with hospital staff, so I stepped out of the room without complaint, though I lingered near the door.

Jason joined me, leaning against the wall just a few feet away as we both listened to the beeping of alarms and whirring of machines that was constant background noise in a hospital.

"Hey," Jason said after a moment, staring daggers at the far wall. "I know it's probably a bit late to say this, but if you ever hurt him, I'll end you if it's the last thing I do." His tone was casual, but the look in his eyes when he glanced at me was as cold and calculating as a viper. "I spent almost eleven years looking for him, so you know how stubborn I can be. You may be law enforcement, but I'll find a way, even if it means burying your body in the woods."

I leaned closer to him so no one else would be able to hear our potentially disturbing conversation.

"If I ever hurt him, I'll beat you to it and put a bullet in my head myself."

Jason nodded, satisfied with my answer, and the two of us reached a silent understanding. We spent the rest of our time waiting without saying another word, positioned to either side of Clay's door like a pair of dedicated guard dogs.

CHAPTER THIRTY

Logan

THE HOSPITAL STAFF decided to keep Clay overnight for observation, just in case. Jason had been allowed to stay with him since they were family, but I'd been booted to the lonely wastelands of a nearby hotel room the minute visiting hours were over.

I returned the next morning, coffee cup in hand and yawning from a poor night's sleep. The hotel had been particularly cheap, and the bed was of such low quality that I may as well have slept on the floor. My eyes were gritty, and I still felt half asleep as I neared Clay's hospital room, which is why I didn't immediately recognize the sound of my own name until I was almost through the door.

I stopped just on the other side of the doorframe, listening to the conversation happening just a few feet away.

"No, I can't," Clay was saying. "That wouldn't be fair to Logan."

The hair on the back of my neck stood up.

What was he talking about?

His voice didn't sound distressed, but he also didn't seem happy.

Was there some problem in our relationship that I didn't know about?

If that was the case, why wouldn't he talk to me about it?

I couldn't see what was happening inside the room, but I recognized Jason's voice.

"I'm not saying you have to do anything right now, Clay, but just think about it. Do the two of you really want to be long-distance forever?"

It was a good thing I'd already finished most of my coffee, because the Styrofoam cup crumpled in my hands when I squeezed it.

Was he trying to convince Clay to

break up with me?

I'd thought Jason and I were on the same page yesterday, but apparently, I'd been wrong. I had half a mind to storm into that room and demand answers, but a masochistic part of me was also curious about what Clay would say. If he agreed with his brother, that was something we needed to know now.

Heartbreak would be inevitable. I was already so in love with Clay that breaking up would devastate me, but if we ended it now maybe we could both walk away without too much damage.

Inside the room, Clay sighed.

"No, of course I don't want to be long-distance. No one wants that. But I don't see any other option right now. His life is there, and mine is here."

"Is it?"

Even without seeing Clay, I could feel his confusion radiating out of the room. It mirrored my own. I also had no idea what Jason was talking about.

Someone inside the room shifted around loud enough for me to hear their fidgeting.

"Clay." Jason said his brother's name like it was a sentence all on its own.

"Think about it. Is your life really here? You live here, yes. But that doesn't mean your life is here. We've been talking recently about your future. Once you get your GED, then you can do anything. Get your own job. Go to college. Spend time traveling. Whatever you want. But none of that has to be here. My life is here, with Patrick. But your life could be anywhere. It could even be in Louisiana."

My breath caught in my lungs when I realized what they were talking about.

Clay moving to Baton Rouge with me?

I'd be a liar if I said I never thought about it, but it had always seemed like a fantasy rather than reality. Clay wouldn't want to leave his brother after finally settling down here.

Would he?

The frustrated groan that Clay let out was very familiar. It was the same sound he made whenever he was studying, and he couldn't figure out the answer to a problem.

"Ugh. I don't know. Baton Rouge is so far away. What would I even do there?"

"The same things you do here. I was the only person you knew when you came here, and you managed to carve out a decent life here. You can do the same thing over there."

"But..." Clay's voice started off strong, but in the course of only three letters, it died to a barely audible whisper. "I was only able to do that because you gave me a place to stay."

"And I'm sure Logan would happily let you live with him as well. In fact, I'll personally knock his teeth out if he doesn't."

Clay laughed, and the music of such a joyous sound distracted me from the topic of the conversation.

"Jason. Stop acting like you're some dangerous street fighter. You've never thrown a punch in your life."

"Never said I'd use my fist. A baseball bat would also work."

Clay laughed again, quieter this time. The rollercoaster that my emotions had been subjected to over the last few minutes finally calmed down, and I realized I was still clutching the crumpled cup. The dregs of my coffee were dripping over my fingers and making a sticky mess, so I threw it in the trashcan and pulled out some tissues from my pocket to try and clean myself up.

All the while, I kept one ear attuned to the conversation happening inside the room.

"I've been saving everything I can from my paychecks," Clay admitted. "You're paying me more than I deserve, so I might be able to afford a few months of rent, but what if I'm not able to find a job there?"

"Is that what you're concerned about?" Jason asked, sounding just as incredulous as I felt. "Clay, maybe I'm wrong, but I get the feeling Logan would gladly let you live without him without asking for rent."

I couldn't stay out of the conversation any longer and poked my head around the door.

"You're absolutely right."

Both men jumped in surprise. Jason just rolled his eyes when he realized I'd been listening in, but Clay's face grew crimson from embarrassment.

"Logan. How long have you been there?"

"Long enough." I reclaimed the same seat I'd been sitting in yesterday and grabbed Clay's hand. "Your brother is right. If you came to Baton Rouge, I absolutely would not demand rent payment from you. Or any other expense, for that matter. You should only focus on figuring out what it is you want to do. Let me worry about the money."

Clay shoved my shoulder but didn't actually put any distance between us. "No. I am not taking advantage of you like that. I'll pay my own way." He seemed to realize that he was already talking about moving to Baton Rouge like it was a done decision, and immediately clammed up. "I, uh, I mean. If I do move in with you. Maybe. I don't know what I'm doing yet."

Jason and I shared a look over Clay's head. We were both thinking the same thing. If Clay was already imagining what life in Baton Rouge would be like, then it was inevitable. We may as well start packing now.

"Okay," I relented and pressed a kiss to his temple. "Once you know what you want to do in the future, let me know. My door is always open for you."

The conversation turned toward other, less emotional topics, but in the back of my mind I was already making plans. There wasn't enough space in my apartment for two people. I'd chosen the apartment because of its proximity to my work, but I wouldn't mind a slightly longer commute if it meant Clay could be more comfortable.

Would Clay want to be near the University?

He was trying to get his GED, so maybe he'd want to continue his education.

Or maybe he'd want to be closer to places he could volunteer, like halfway houses and children's shelters. He enjoyed his volunteer work here in Maryland and would probably want to continue with it.

While Clay was distracted talking with his brother about something, I discreetly pulled up apartment listings on my phone. It was too early to actually move anywhere, but there was no harm in making plans for the future.

Our future.

I couldn't keep the smile off my face just thinking about it.

CHAPTER THIRTY-ONE

Clay

TWO YEARS AFTER we met, I stepped into Logan's apartment for the first time.

No, it was my apartment. I lived here now.

It was new for Logan as well, as his place hadn't been big enough for two people. We'd picked it out together online, but Logan had gone to visit the place alone, so I'd never seen it in person before.

Moving so far across the country while also getting ready to take the GED test had been a nightmare to manage. I'd had more than one meltdown in the ensuing months, which Logan had talked me through over the phone. There were some days I didn't think I'd ever get here, but here we were. The results of my GED test had just come in a few days ago, and while I didn't ace it, my score was more than enough to pass.

Jason and Patrick had thrown me a graduation party, which also doubled as a going-away party. The house had been covered in so much confetti, they were still finding it in the couch cushions when I left.

The bags I was carrying hit the ground with a loud thud as I looked around the living room of my new home. Most of my stuff was being shipped separately, so my bags only held the basic essentials.

When I'd arrived at my brother's place two years ago, I'd had only a single bag's worth of stuff to my name. Now, I'd acquired so much stuff, it required special shipping.

What a difference two years could make.

Strong arms wrapped around me from behind, and Logan's warm body pressed up against my back. It was another testament to my progress that I didn't jump or flinch from the unexpected contact, and merely relaxed back into the embrace.

Logan's lips skimmed the side of my neck before he spoke directly into my ear.

"So, what'd you think of the place?"

I looked around for a moment, as if I hadn't just been admiring the space around me.

"I don't know. Did we really need such a big place? I can't even help with the rent until I get a job. Maybe three bedrooms was too much."

I laughed, but it wasn't a joke. The price tag on a three-bedroom apartment in the middle of Baton Rouge was no laughing matter. We'd argued over it for weeks, especially when Logan tried to insist that I didn't need to pay for anything. We eventually compromised when Logan pointed out that we needed the space. His job, especially after his promotion, required a secure home office. Plus, it wouldn't be right to ask my brother and Patrick to sleep on the couch when they came to visit. So, a guestroom was also a necessity.

I'd agreed to the three bedrooms on the condition that I paid at least a small portion of the rent.

My savings wouldn't allow me to pay much right now, but I was determined to one day afford my half of the rent.

Once I figured out what career path I wanted to pursue. I didn't have all the answers yet, but there was time to figure it out.

I looked over my shoulder at Logan, making sure to smile at him so he would know I was joking about the apartment.

He just shook his head and gave me a brief kiss.

"Tease."

Before he could get too far away, I slipped a hand into his hair and pulled him back into a proper kiss.

Sexual frustration was a new experience. I'd never really desired anyone before Logan, and for most of our relationship, sex had been a difficult subject. Finally, after two years of therapy, I was comfortable enough to admit that I wanted him without any guilt.

Unfortunately, despite this breakthrough, he'd remained frustratingly out of reach. We'd been so busy the last few months, there hadn't been much time for romance. Even the number of intimate video calls had decreased.

Even now, with him standing so close to me that I could feel the heat of his body through our clothes, desire pumped through my veins. We'd nearly joined the mile-high club on the flight over here. The only thing that stopped me was the fact that Logan was the one flying the plane.

Now that we had our feet on the ground, I wasn't going to wait any longer.

When the kiss ended, I turned around and looped both arms around his neck.

"The living room looks great, but I'm more interested in the bedroom."

Logan's dark eyes sparked, and he led me by the hand through the bedroom door.

"Here. Take a look. I tried to decorate it in a way I thought you'd like, but feel free to change anything you want."

I couldn't have recalled a single detail about the bedroom if someone had asked me about it later. All I saw was the bed, illuminated by a single ray of afternoon sunlight that snuck through a tiny gap in the closed curtains.

Tossing my jacket onto a nearby chair, I sat on the edge of the bed. "It's perfect."

I'd hoped that my invitation would be obvious, but Logan didn't seem to be getting the hint. He stayed standing by the door, rocking back and forth on the balls of his feet.

"That's good. I've kept half the drawers empty, so you can move your stuff in whenever. We can also reorganize things if you—"

"Logan," I cut off his rambling. "That all sounds great, but it's really not what I'm interested in right now."

I held out my hand toward him, making my invitation clearer, but he still didn't come any closer.

"What, um..." He cleared his throat, looking as nervous as a teenager about to ask their crush to prom. "What are you interested in?"

Was he playing coy?

Is that what was happening here?

Every person I'd ever slept with before had approached sex with a single-minded purpose. I'd never had to invite someone into bed before. My compliance was already assumed by the time we got this far.

For once, remembering my past didn't hurt. It still wasn't pleasant, but it wasn't the instant mood killer it used to be.

Logan and I had done plenty of stuff together over video calls.

Why was it so much more awkward in person?

Thinking back to those calls, I realized what was different. Every time we'd gotten sexual before, I had usually taken the initiative and told Logan what to do. Yet now that we were finally face to face, I expected him to take the lead because that was what always happened in the past.

That wouldn't do.

Adopting a more confident set to my shoulders, I leaned back on my hands and pointedly glanced at the floor in front of me.

"Logan. Get over here."

Just as I'd hoped, he jumped to my command. His knees hit the floor so quickly as he knelt in front of me that I could feel the impact even through the carpet. Thank God he was in good shape, or he would have hurt himself.

Taking command over a video call was one thing, but doing it in person was a much greater challenge. I felt like a fraud. My veneer of confidence was only paper thin, but before I could second guess myself, I hooked one leg over his shoulder and pulled him closer.

"That's better. I was started to feel like you'd lost interest in me."

He ran his hands up both my legs from ankle to thigh, stopping just before he reached the crease of my hip. "No. I want to make sure I'm not pressuring you into anything. And..." His cheeks turned bright red, and he buried his face against my thigh to hide his expression. "And it's really hot when you order me around."

I tangled my hand in his hair, giving me a perfect handle to tip his head up and make him look at me.

"Doing this over video is one thing, but you still like it when we're in-person?"

He nodded, accidentally tugging his own hair.

"More than like it. I love it. Tell me what you want me to do."

The desperation in his eyes, and the way his breathing picked up just from thinking about following my orders, sent a thrill of arousal through me. I could get used to this.

"Ah, Logan." I sighed as I tightened my hand in his hair. "You're going to spoil me. All right. You want me to tell you what to do? Fine."

I pushed down on his head just hard enough for him to feel it.

"These last few weeks have been so stressful. Make me feel good so I can relax."

The power I felt when he instantly moved to obey me was thrilling. First placing several kisses along my inner thigh, he worked his way upward until he was literally nuzzling between my legs. Even just the pressure I could feel through my pants was pleasurable. I couldn't imagine how good skin-on-skin contact would feel, but I was eager to find out.

Logan quickly grew frustrated with the barrier my pants created and reenacted some of his dirtier dreams by pulling the zipper down with his teeth. I had to stop him and remove my pants myself for fear that he would rip my clothing, but eventually, I sat there in nothing but a button-down shirt that was left hanging completely open.

With my hand in Logan's hair, I guided him back where I wanted him. We both moaned when his lips brushed over my arousal. It was a strange sensation to be touched there so delicately. Even my own hand wasn't as gentle. Logan's lips, followed by his tongue, were as delicate as a butterfly's wing.

I tipped my head back and closed my eyes, intending to enjoy the sensation, but in the darkness behind my eyelids, other memories started playing. My eyes immediately sprang back open and I looked back down at Logan, reminding myself who was touching me now.

It wasn't the same.

Nothing about this was the same, and I refused to ruin this moment by letting those old memories overlap with my new reality.

Using his hair like puppet strings, I directed the motion of his head.

"Come on. Don't tease me. Make me feel good."

After taking a deep breath, Logan wrapped his mouth around me and swallowed me whole. My hand that wasn't in his hair fisted in the bed sheet as I cried out from the shocking sensation that ran along my entire nervous system.

His mouth serviced me with the confidence of a pro. I would have been jealous of the people he'd gotten on his knees for in the past if I could have formed a complete thought, but the only words running through my brain were "More. More. Yes. Please. More."

I may have also been saying them out loud, but I couldn't tell through the static that filled my ears.

As I felt my climax approaching, my back arched and my hips jerked, driving me deeper into his throat. Logan didn't even choke as he accepted all of me and sped up. My hand still sat on his head, riding the up and down motion rather than guiding it.

I could have told him to stop at any time. I wouldn't even need to use words. A simple tug at his hair would be enough to get my point across, and I knew he'd immediately stop the moment I did.

This thought, more than anything, drove me over the edge. My toes curled into the carpet, and I whined in the back of my throat like a dying animal as I came.

Logan showed off his surprising talent by swallowing most of what I gave him. He didn't even look embarrassed when he gazed up at me with the evidence of my pleasure glistening on his lips. In that moment, if anyone was asked to guess which of us had been paid for sex before, Logan would have seemed like the better candidate than me.

"Fuck," I gasped as I collapsed back against the bed. "I want to ask where you learned to do that, but I'm afraid of the answer."

Now Logan dared to look embarrassed, sitting back on his heels and staring down at the floor like he'd done something wrong.

"Oh, no." I grabbed his chin and tipped his head up. "Don't go getting bashful on me now. There's a story behind that. What it is?"

Clearing his throat, Logan wiped his lips and chin with the back of his hand. His mumbled answer was so quiet I had to ask him to repeat himself, and even then, I struggled to hear what he said.

"You, um, aren't the first sex worker I've dated. They taught me some things."

A brief flicker of jealousy alighted in my heart, but it died almost immediately. I couldn't blame anyone for wanting to date Logan. He was too perfect to pass up. I was just glad that this unnamed ex had left him free and available for me.

"Remind me to send this ex of yours a thank you card."

Logan still knelt on the floor at my feet, his own arousal unsated and straining against the confines of his pants. He didn't say anything about it, but I knew it was driving him crazy from the way he kept shifting his legs.

I took my time removing my shirt, the last piece of clothing I still wore, and shuffled up to the top of the bed where I made myself comfortable among the pillows.

Still, Logan didn't move from his place. He didn't even try to stroke himself through his pants. He just sat there, enduring the desperation, as he waited for my next order.

I was half-tempted to leave him wanting. There was something dark and thrilling about the thought of getting him riled up and then refusing to give him any relief.

Maybe we could play with that idea another day. I had a feeling Logan would find it just as enjoyable as I did.

Not today, though.

Today was a day for both of us to

enjoy.

I curled my hand toward myself, beckoning him over. "Get undressed and come here."

Logan practically tore his clothes from his body. I was genuinely surprised I didn't hear ripping fabric as I watched him toss them aside. He climbed onto the bed with me but hesitated before touching me.

In response, I spread my legs to make room for him.

He still hesitated. "Are you sure? We can do it the other way if you'd prefer."

I'd never actually considered that before. My role in bed had always been assumed. Doing it any other way had never occurred to me as a possibility.

Thinking about it for a second, I shook my head.

"Maybe another time. For now, I want it like this."

He was still obviously hesitant, so I grabbed his shoulders and guided him forward until he knelt over me with his hands planted on the bed near my head and my legs wrapped around his hips.

I ran gentle hands over his shoulders and down his back, admiring the strong but safe cage his body formed around me.

"Everything with you has felt so different than what I've known before. I want to know how different this will feel as well. I need to feel you inside me."

The nightstand beside the bed was close enough for Logan to reach without leaving me. He tossed a bottle of lubricant onto the mattress beside me, then held up a condom with a question in his eyes.

I debated with myself, but ultimately shook my head. "Do you mind if we don't use it. I'm clean. I promise. Jason insisted I get tested for everything possible, and I haven't slept with anyone since. I just... I really want to feel you as much as possible."

Logan tossed the condom aside without protest. "I'm clean as well. I got tested just last week. Not because I thought there was a problem, but just because I wanted to be able to prove it to you. I can get the paperwork, if you want to see it."

I held on tight to his shoulders before he could leave.

"It's all right. I believe you. But thanks for making so much effort. You didn't have to do that. I would have believed you even without proof."

He pressed a heartbreakingly tender kiss to my forehead.

"I just want to make sure you're comfortable."

I held back the tears that wanted to well up in my eyes and gave him a smile instead. "I promise you. I'm very comfortable." Then I handed him the bottle of lube. "Now, get to work."

Logan's fingers slid into me easily. Two years of celibacy wasn't enough to make me forget how sex worked, and I found it very easy to relax while holding onto him and breathing in his comforting scent.

While he slowly stretched me open, Logan pressed dozens of kisses over my neck and chest. His fingers sought every pleasurable spot inside of me until I was a writhing, desperate mess.

"I'm ready," I gasped as his fingers pushed even deeper. "I was ready a while ago. Now, you're just trying to make me beg."

Logan just laughed and kissed me again. "Patience. There's nothing wrong with making sure you enjoy it."

"Enjoy" was an understatement. Logan's touch was so different from anything else I'd ever experienced, there was no comparison.

When he finally deemed me ready—and when I was nearly clawing at him in desperation—he removed his fingers and hitched my legs higher around his waist to line himself up.

My fingernails left crescents on his shoulders as he pushed inside me. I couldn't help the instinct that made me want to brace for pain. Yet, I felt nothing but pleasure and satisfaction as he buried himself deep inside me. At this point, I may as well call myself a virgin. If this was what being with someone was supposed to be like, then everything I'd experienced before shouldn't even count as sex.

Logan started moving, soft and shallow at first, but quickly gaining strength. I clung to him, crying out in ecstasy with each thrust. He must have really been paying attention when he used his fingers, because he managed to hit my deepest pleasure spot with deadly accuracy every time.

I couldn't take it. I wasn't used to feeling so much all at once. Yet, at the same time I didn't want him to stop.

I wrapped my arms and legs around him as tightly as I could, practically merging our bodies together as I mumbled encouragement into his ear.

"Fuck. Baby, just like that. So good. You're so good."

With each thrust, Logan sent me higher and higher until it almost felt like I'd slipped into the Midnight Zone again. I was barely inside my body anymore, as though my soul was leaking out and filling the air around us.

I could have stayed there forever and lived a happy life.

Eventually, Logan's movements grew more erratic. He was desperately close to his end. Considering how much I'd teased him before this, it was a miracle he'd lasted so long.

His hand slipped between us and started stroking my cock, hastening my own climax so I could join him. He was mumbling something into my ear the whole time, and though I couldn't make out the words through the pounding of my own heartbeat, the sound of his voice was enough to tickle the back of my brain.

I bit his shoulder when I came. I didn't

plan to do so. It just happened in the heat of the moment.

He grunted in shock from the unexpected pain, but just held me closer as he reached his own end.

Subtle warmth spread inside me as his hips stuttered, and I could just make out the sound of him repeating my name over and over.

Was there something better than heaven?

If so, then this was it.

When it ended, and we'd both calmed down enough to at least give each other breathing room, Logan lay on his back with his head on a pillow and one arm still around me. I let my head rest on his shoulder, hooking one leg around his hips to keep him close, and basked in the warmth radiating off him.

I'd heard people describe a "post-sex afterglow" but never experienced it myself until now. It was another first I could give Logan. I wondered if I'd ever stop discovering new experiences with him, or if he'd spend the rest of our lives surprising me.

The thought startled me. While I'd been contemplating the future recently,

I'd never thought so far ahead to use phrases like "the rest of my life".

I found I enjoyed the thought a lot more than I expected. So long as Logan was there, I'd probably enjoy anything.

Propping my chin on his chest, I looked up at him.

"I was thinking of taking some classes."

His eyes still weren't fully focused, and he struggled to comprehend what I was saying at first.

"What? You mean, like, at the University?"

"Yeah." I lazily drew nonsense symbols over his chest with one of my fingers. "I still have no idea what I'd want to major in, or if college is even the right choice for me, but I thought maybe I could take some of the core classes while I decided."

He squeezed my shoulder in a one-armed hug. "That's a great idea. I'm sure you've already discussed this with Jason, but if you need help paying for classes, feel free to ask me."

I nodded but didn't respond. I'd already gone through this song and dance with Jason, and I'd given up trying to convince either of them to save their money.

At this rate, my brother and my boyfriend were going to end up fighting over who got to pay for me.

Shifting onto his side so he could see me better, Logan braced his head on his hand. "While I'm glad to hear you've got plans, what brought this on?"

I shrugged. "Just... thinking about the future."

We lay there in silence for a moment, listening to each other's heartbeats, but eventually, Logan let out a deep sigh and sat up.

"That reminds me of something else I need to talk to you about. This probably isn't the best time, but I didn't think there is a good time, so may as well do it now."

He sounded serious, so I sat up as well. While we'd been busy, the sunlight sneaking through the curtain had turned to moonlight, and the air between us was aglow with silver dust.

"What is it?" I placed a hand on his knee and scooted closer until I was practically in his lap. "You can tell me anything. I promise I won't get upset."

Well, that was probably a lie. I wasn't always the best at regulating my emotions, but I would give it my best try.

Looking at me up and down like he was judging the validity of my claim, Logan sighed again.

"You know I've been building a case against Preston Vanshaw ever since you told me about him."

Every muscle in my body grew tense, but I didn't pull away. "Yeah. What about it?"

"I was hoping it wouldn't come to this, but making a case against him isn't going to be easy. This whole operation is good at hiding their tracks. If we're going to have any chance of putting these bastards away, then we're going to need as much proof as possible, and... and it's going to be nearly impossible without a witness."

He didn't say it directly, but I knew what he was asking.

"You need me to testify."

For a moment, it looked like he was going to argue. His mouth opened and the words were on the tip of his tongue, but then he just silently nodded.

Telling my therapist and Logan about what happened to me was hard enough. I hadn't even told my brother most of the details.

Would I be able to tell my story to a room full of strangers?

I didn't know a lot about the legal process, but I was pretty sure they were going to want me to be as detailed and specific as possible.

"I'll do it."

"What?" Logan grabbed my hands and squeezed them almost hard enough to hurt. "Clay. Wait. Take some time to think about it."

I pulled my hands away, and snuggled myself into the circle of his arms instead so he was holding my entire body.

"I've been doing nothing but thinking about it for two years. Hell, for my whole life. Nothing will get better just because I keep it to myself."

I could feel his hesitation even without looking up at him.

"If you're sure."

"I'm not." I hid my face against his chest. "But I think I'm ready to try."

Logan's arms were like a security blanket as they held me tight. "I should warn you, testifying won't be the end. If anything, it'll be the beginning of our fight. Cases like this take a long time and a lot of effort to resolve."

"I know. I'm ready."

This time, I managed to say it with more conviction.

The heavy moment was interrupted by a loud protest from my stomach. I'd been too busy to each much today, and after my recent exertion, my stomach had apparently decided to put its foot down.

Groaning, I collapsed onto the bed and tucked my head under the pillows. "I'm hungry, but I'm too tired to get up. Do you think my stomach will shut up if I just ignore it?"

I felt the mattress jostle as Logan moved, but instead of joining me, he left the bed entirely.

"I said I'd do whatever you told me. That includes orders from your stomach as well. I'll put a meal together for us. Don't worry. I stocked the fridge before you came. I remember your appetite."

His footsteps moved away, but suddenly stopped near the door. I peeked out from under the pillow to find him standing there, smiling at me.

"I just realized I forgot to say something earlier."

Pulling my head completely out from under the pillows, I looked at him with confusion. "What?"

His smile grew even wider. "Welcome home."

Then he left and a moment later I heard him moving around in the kitchen.

Rolling onto my back, I stared at the ceiling and watched the movement of the moonlight as I listened to Logan humming to himself as he cooked for us.

"I'm ready."

Dear Reader,

Thank you for reading Logan & Clay's story.

As hard as it is to believe, child trafficking is a huge issue in our country. While Clay's story is obviously fiction, the premise is way too real. Sadly, most children who are abducted and sold into this disgusting slavery never make it home. In fact, too few are ever even found.

We *can* make a difference, though. If you see something that doesn't seem quite right, make a stink and call your local police. Better to risk an overreaction than to find out later a child you saw fighting with his "uncle" was truly kidnapped. All it takes is one person to make a difference. Above all, though, be safe.

Oh, and if you enjoyed this book, maybe you'll do me a huge favor and leave a review. Even a few words would mean the world to me, and it also helps other readers find the stories you love.

Thanks!

~Evie Riley

OTHER BOOKS BY EVIE

Federal Protection Agency

Mason

Rafe

Ryzen

Cooper

Noah

Damien

Sebastian

Gabe

Logan

Ruthless Empire

Courting Danger

Chasing Danger

Kissing Danger

Smokejumpers

Hawke

Cyrus

Jase

Gage

Jackson

Xavier

EVIE RILEY

Jasper Springs
Cade
Dawson
Drew
Grayson
Riley
Mitch

From The Edge
Shattered
Runaway
Jaded
Rescue
Hidden
Tormented

Gray Vale Pack
His Fated Mate
His Wounded Warrior
His Healing Heart

ABOUT THE AUTHOR

Evie Riley is a prolific, neurodivergent author known for her captivating MM romance novels. She has gained a significant following and topped the LGBT+ action and adventure bestseller charts with her series.

Evie's writing style often explores dark and gritty themes where her men must overcome difficult obstacles in their search for love, but she has also ventured into sweeter small-town romances, incorporating tropes like enemies-to-lovers, friends-to-lovers, age-gap, and forced proximity. She is known for crafting engaging romantic suspense novels and has a knack for creating interconnected series worlds that keep readers invested.

Interestingly, Ms. Riley has hinted at exploring new genres, such as Alien Omegaverse Romance, in the future.

Outside of writing, she enjoys spending time at the beach and has a quirky personality, described by her partner as ranging from cute to deadly, depending on her blood-chocolate levels.

Evie spends her nights writing bad boys in love, and her days wrangling the sweet boys she loves.